Redemption

Redemption
A Jo Walker Mystery

Karen Starkins

Edited by Don Metzler and Leah Naess

Print layout, e-book conversion, and cover design by DLD Books Editing and Self-Publishing Services

DLD Books
www.dldbooks.com

Copyright 2022 by Karen Starkins
All rights reserved

Cover photograph by Leah Naess
Cover design by David Dvorkin

ISBN: 979-8-9873582-0-7

First edition: October 4, 2023

Audio book: Production copyright 2023 By Karen Starkins
ISBN: 979-8-9873582-2-1

Paperback: Production copyright 2023 By Karen Starkins
ISBN: 979-8-9873582-0-7

Hardback: Production copyright 2023 By Karen Starkins
ISBN: 979-8-9873582-3-8

Large print: Production copyright 2023 By Karen Starkins
ISBN: 979-8-9873582-4-5

Prologue

Angela stepped forward, hurrying down the alley and out across the street. She stopped two blocks away from the cathedral. The late news tumbled in muted voices from apartment buildings nearby. Doors slammed as waiters carried the last of the trash to the alley dumpsters. The city was closing for the night. Time was slipping away from her. Yet still she huddled immobile against a wall in the darkness just beyond the circle of light cast by a street light.

Blue–white light pulsated from each passing car. A couple approached along the sidewalk. She edged forward. They were old, older even than her mother and father, she thought. They talked softly, leaning into each other. The girl ached to run to them begging help. She took a tentative step forward, barely touching the ring of light, her body still, in shadow, only her face lit by the streetlight. She folded her arms around her slender frame. She stood mute. She didn't know the language. The plea tumbled through her in the fluid waves of her native tongue. But it did not escape her.

The girl watched from the dark as her chance slid by in soft voices. It was her only chance, but she didn't know that. She still hoped she would find help at the cathedral, visible now, silhouetted by the city lights. In her home, the church was a place of refuge. The men that took her, they said no one would help her if she ran, that the Americans didn't care. They would throw her in prison. But wasn't God the same here as He was at home? The priests would help her.

Even if the priests couldn't help, she had his phone. She could make a trade with it. Its owner would want it back, desperately, she thought. It was dangerous, she knew. She had taken pictures with it and she had stolen it. To get it back he would help her. He bragged of how powerful he was. And she believed him because she saw how the other men treated him. But she knew full well that she would need someone else's help to negotiate the trade. She couldn't do it by herself.

She stepped out between two parked cars. She thought she heard scuffing steps behind her. But when she looked, there was only the dark alley.

Ahead on the next street corner was a blue mailbox, squat and ugly under a dim streetlight. In her mind she made this a temporary goal, to reach this mailbox . . . a waypoint on her desperate journey.

She was nearly breathless by the time she came to the box, and leaned against it, panting for air. Then she brushed past it and moved on.

Moments later she was running up to the cathedral steps. She crouched beside a young tree. Barren of leaves, it offered no cover. She feared the bright lights that lit the cathedral entrance. She was close, so close.

She gathered her courage for a final push and sprinted up the concrete steps. She grabbed the handle of the giant golden door and pulled. It didn't move. She pulled again. Still it didn't open. In rising panic she ran from one door to the next pulling frantically on each. None opened. She heard a soft scuffle back from where she had crossed the street. Panicked, she ran, away from the cathedral, away from the sound. She was in a small garden that nestled against the cathedral's eastern side. She ran past a statue of Mary, the Virgin's arms translucent in the dim light, lifting toward heaven in supplication. The girl prayed to Mary as she ran. Or was it to her own mother that she cried out? Anyone, anyone who would offer salvation from what pursued her.

She heard him running behind her as she exited the garden. She didn't turn to look and didn't call out again for help. She just ran breathless and sobbing. She was halfway across the parking lot when he caught her, grabbing her throat from behind. She felt her head jerk as he yanked her backwards, his fingers clawing into the soft skin of her neck, twisting her head. She passed out seconds before her neck snapped.

Chapter One

Dorothea Messenger, Dottie to her friends and supporters, stepped from the podium into a welcoming surge of handshakes and praise. Her aide, Jacob Shaw, ran interference like a fox terrier. He bolted from side to side, a snarl on his face, a glare in his eyes, guarding his mistress from strangers and unwelcome guests. I was one of those unwelcome guests. If I ventured too close, Shaw would be sure to bite. And he'd be sure to enjoy it. Not only was I part of the accursed fake news media, I reported for a regional paper well-known for its liberal bent. I kept to my seat near the back of the room, watching, waiting for a chance to approach Messenger when Shaw's guard was down.

Messenger's keynote speech to the Conference for Immigration Reform had brought out a mixed crowd. Men dressed for business in clean-pressed suits and muted silk ties traded nods with combat fatigue-clad teenagers and oldsters who never outgrew their combat fantasies. Former U.S. Congressman Rich Hardy, national standard bearer for immigration reform, stood behind the podium muttering comments to his wife.

Messenger smiled to one and all, a queen giving benediction to her subjects. The audience loved the speech, and that disturbed me as much as the message.

Not long ago Messenger's speech would have branded her a racist and a dangerous extremist. Now she was the darling of

Colorado's conservative coalition. Today a congresswoman, tomorrow a senator. And, if this crowd had its way, Messenger would be in the next presidential primaries.

When she accused illegal immigrants of stealing jobs from deserving Americans, the audience cheered. When she said illegal immigrants brought crime to Colorado, they cheered louder. When she spoke softly of the threat to our American way of life and to national security, the crowd stirred and muttered. When she threw her support behind a state proposition to deny even emergency health services to illegals, they nodded with satisfaction. And when she praised the brave men who set up their own defense of America's borders, she brought the audience to their feet.

Beside her, Jim Duffet stood through the speech beaming like a kid with his first crush. Duffet was the head honcho of Coloradoans for Immigration Reform. I couldn't think of a single good thing about the man. He's slick as wet ice and has the moral compass of a psychopath. Usually his fellow activists make him sit in the back of the class so he isn't overheard proclaiming the onset of Armageddon. Clearly he was moving up the political ladder. He was standing beside Messenger, the reigning monarch.

With the speech finally over, I was trying to decide if it was worth the effort to push through the adoring crowd to pressure Messenger into an impromptu interview. Then I heard my name.

"Hey Walker, what brings you to the enemy camp?"

I turned to see Russ Rigby walking my way. Russ works for the local daily paper. He's not exactly a competitor. Still our friendship is marked more by distrust than cooperation. Russ is a crime reporter, so maybe distrust is just part of his job.

"I'm doing some background for a story on immigration. How about you? I'll agree a crime's been committed here this morning, but not one I'd expect you to be covering."

Russ came toward me through the crowd, edging between two

men engaged in a heated debate about the comparative merits of deportation and incarceration: deport them and they don't pay for their crime, they'll just come back; incarcerate them and you don't get rid of them. Neither man seemed to care much about the merits of the other's opinion, but they clearly were enjoying the argument.

Russ came to stand beside me. He is a tall man with the build of a greyhound, all length and no girth. Even though he towered over me, I felt sure if I leaned against him we'd both topple over.

He smiled. "The editor needed someone to cover this sideshow and I was the last one left standing when everyone dove under their desks."

"Gotta work on that reaction time."

"No kidding. So, really, Jo, what are you doing here? *The Review* never met a conservative cause it liked. There's got to be some story here, but I'm not hearing anything new."

Russ looked at me with a smile I'm sure he meant to convey the friendly support of comrades in a common cause. I just saw the greyhound starting to salivate. This was a man hungry for a story in a wasteland of jingoism and cliché. I wasn't feeling sympathetic. If I was going to shovel through the muck to find an angle, Russ could do his own digging. Messenger just didn't bring out the altruist in me.

"Sorry Russ, you're on your own with this one. I've got nothing."

Russ didn't look convinced. But if there was some scoop waiting to astound the public, I wasn't seeing it.

I picked up my notes and headed for the door.

Messenger was long gone in a cloud of supporters, which suited me fine. I wasn't much up for wrestling the beast, having heard it snarl.

Chapter Two

I stepped out into the bracing, chill air of a late April day in the Mile High city. The downtown streets were teeming with pedestrians, cyclists, and an occasional horse-drawn carriage.

I'd lived my high school years in Boulder, just a half hour's drive north. But college and career had taken me to the East coast in search of journalist fame, or notoriety. What I'd gotten instead was bruised and distressed enough to send me home to Colorado.

I'd last spent time in Denver 20 years ago when I interned at *The Review* during summer breaks from NYU. When I returned to live here a year ago, I'd barely recognized the place. Downtown was changing, from factories to loft apartments, department stores to boutiques, Levis and cowboy boots to designer jeans and stiletto heels.

I was still trying to decide if I liked the new look and feel. The restaurants and book stores were great. The traffic was a pain, parking impossible. All in all I couldn't help feeling that the Botox treatment smoothed out some of the character. Still, character isn't always fun to live with. And it's nice to get spruced up once in a while.

I picked up my car, cleared downtown and headed to *The Review* offices on Bannock Street in a part of town that hasn't yet been overrun by the spreading face-lift.

The offices of *The Review* are buried in a lump of pink cement that fails utterly in its attempt to mimic an adobe hacienda. In recognition of the failed impersonation, the sheltered entry has been euphemistically dubbed the courtyard gardens by the resident collection of glib-lipped journalists. It serves as lunch or meeting room on warm days, smokers' retreat in any weather. There's bicycle parking, storage for spare furniture, and a pair of kayaks someone left to winter in the gardens but never retrieved. It's a good thing we don't get many visitors; getting to the front door is a triathlon event.

As for the garden label, well I've never seen a living plant in or around the building. As a rule, journalists are not very good with plants. Every reporter in a room will rivet if a politician twitches an eyebrow. But our dinner could be going up in flames in the room next door and we'd still be watching that eyebrow twitch. It's just a question of priorities. Great for gathering news, but hard on plants, pets, and car maintenance.

Today the courtyard was free of human obstacles. I maneuvered through the stationary debris into the lobby.

The lobby is completely filled by a gray government-issue steel desk that was acquired from an army surplus sale, an odd choice for a group of anti-war pacifists. The desk hasn't been staffed since it was crammed into the undersized room 25 years ago. It's not just that *The Review* could never afford a receptionist, which is true. But the paper's founders couldn't make themselves hire someone to sit in a windowless, 100-square-foot room with only a telephone and typewriter for company. Every discussion of the possibility ended in heated arguments about third-world sweat shops and 19th century labor revolts. The paper was like that in its early years. The personnel were political and we took everything very personally.

So there was no receptionist. The rare visitor to the paper was greeted by the battered gray desk and a large oak-framed picture of the three people who started the paper. In the picture the three are perched on squat granite boulders in a field of blooming alpine wildflowers. Behind them, Long's Peak spreads the width of the photograph. This picture, or one like it, is a mandatory decoration for any Colorado endeavor from politics to selling hot dogs at baseball games. Nobody is anybody without that mountain mojo.

What I like about this particular rendition of the Colorado moment is that the three people look like they were actually enjoying it, caught off guard in a moment of laughter, just three friends playing in the mountains, enjoying the day. On the left Annie McIntyre is sitting with her mouth open in a wide laugh, her arms flung apart, her left hand casting a lined shadow across Ed's face. Ed Turner is sitting erect in the middle, smiling tentatively, squinting at the camera. Jeff Artis on the right has a hand resting on Ed's knee and is leaning in as if caught in the telling of a good, if scandalous joke.

These were the people who started the paper. These were the people who first taught me my trade when I came on board as a reporter wanna-be. Seeing the picture, I still smile and say a silent good morning to each of them. Working with a group of inexperienced, opinionated, uncompromising, Watergate-inspired, crusading neophytes, these three built *The Review* into a nationally acclaimed regional newspaper.

Of course things changed. Jeff was sucked off into the world of television news in DC. Anne married Ed and left most of the newspaper work to him while she burrowed her way into Denver party politics. So Ed was left at the center of things, running the paper with an increasingly squint-eyed stare.

He was the reason I'd spent my morning with Dorothea Messenger and her crowd. He was also the reason I'd driven down to the office.

Ed was seriously annoyed with the anti-immigrant sentiment

in the country. And when Ed is annoyed he spreads the aggravation around. I was the foot soldier in his current crusade. It was my job to round up the suspects, expose the culprits, and bring justice to the world. But the way I figure, that doesn't mean that I don't get to complain. After my morning at the rally, I was ready to give Ed an earful.

I wove my way through the labyrinth of cubicles that filled the office interior. Ed's office was against the back wall. His door was partially ajar, so I knocked lightly and walked directly in. Ed was seated at his computer scowling.

"I can't believe the idiot declared war!"

In other circumstances this might be an alarming statement, but I'd had some experience with Ed and his computer. Ed had resisted computers like a cat resists a bath, all yowls and slashing claws. Even when he'd finally agreed to computerize the rest of the office, he'd clung to his Selectric, his tether to a vanishing age.

Then, Ed discovered computer games. Not card games or shoot'em up games. Ed and several hundred of his closest computer buddies were building Utopia in cyberspace.

I suspect that reform in the physical world had gotten a bit too frustrating for Ed in the Trump years. A good computerized fantasy seemed a harmless substitute. But it wasn't going well in Utopia. Utopia had just gone to war.

Ed turned from the computer with a grunt that spoke worlds of his disgust with humanity in general.

My plans for an outraged tirade evaporated. It just didn't seem right to kvetch at the man when his virtual reality was going up in a nuclear storm.

"Just thought I'd let you know I was back in the office in case you had anything for me."

I could see his mind click back to terra firma. He shuffled through the papers on his desk and handed me a news clipping.

"As a matter of fact, I do. I want you to look into this. It's from today's *Post*. It may fit in with the immigration story. Give you a good handle for the piece."

It was brief and didn't provide many details. A young Latina woman had been found with a broken neck near the bike path that ran along the South Platte. Her face disfigured, no identification. The police were investigating.

"What makes you think it's related to the immigration story?"

He frowned, shaking his head. "Something doesn't fit. Based on the way the woman was dressed, the makeup, all that, the official police line is that she was a prostitute who picked up the wrong meal ticket. At least that's what they are investigating. But I've talked to some guys at the department who see it differently. There were racial slurs spray-painted at the scene." He hesitated.

"Some nasty stuff. The police are chalking it up to intentional misdirection . . . some guy who thinks he can hide behind the immigration uproar. Not everyone is convinced. I'm not convinced. So, that's your assignment. Convince me or find out what's going on."

I stared at Ed's desk, not wanting him to read the images that haunted me. This was not an assignment that I wanted. I had moved back to Colorado to escape the death I'd seen in Boston. The death I'd caused. Unintentional, but still I didn't absolve myself. The last thing I wanted was to look back into that abyss.

"I don't do murders Ed, you know that," I said.

Ed knew my history, but his scowl didn't reek of sympathy.

"Look, Jo, you can let your past rule you or you can get on with your job. I expect the latter. I'm not asking you to investigate the murder and certainly not to solve it. But if there is some lunatic out there shooting people just for being Latino, I want enough evidence to stop the police from burying it as some common street crime. Just check out the motivation."

"Okay, I can do that much as long as that's all you want. But why would the police brush off evidence like that?"

"It's complicated. This city's been getting a bad rap recently about immigration," he said. "Messenger and her crowd are harassing the mayor about making Denver too safe for illegals. You know, the whole sanctuary city thing. The police don't like it. Makes it sound like they're not doing their job. Then the Latino community is up in arms about the new immigration restrictions and racial profiling. It's a powder keg. As far as the police are concerned, this is just another murder. Nothing racial about it. They want to keep it low key."

I picked up the article and stood to leave. "I'll see what I can find out."

"It's not going to be easy, Jo. You'll have a hard time finding people willing to talk with you."

I nodded and left his office. A plan was forming, and better not to share it with the boss. He wouldn't approve.

Chapter Three

I was sitting at my desk plotting when renewed inspiration walked up in the form of a 6'2" bright-eyed, bushy-haired intern. Skye hangs around my office a lot, that is, when he's not following me around. He's imprinted. I'm the hotshot reporter returned from success in the metropolis of Boston; he's the cub reporter sidekick. I'm Superman; he's Jimmy Olsen. It isn't easy being Superman, and I've been known to hide in the women's room when Skye shows up. But if I told him we were going to fly to my secret Fortress of Solitude in the Arctic, he'd go pack his parka. That's the dedication I would need for my plan.

I snagged Skye and pulled him into a conference room, closing the door firmly behind us. Not everyone in the office thinks I'm the best influence on Skye. I thought it best to keep our fabrication behind closed doors.

I'd been trying for days to get an appointment with Jim Duffet, the founder of Coloradoans for Immigration Reform. It was an interview I would have preferred to skip. Duffet was near the top of my list of people-who-should-never-be-allowed-to-speak much less have a voice in the immigration debate. Still, my intent had been to use him as a source for the anti-immigration viewpoint for my story. The faction he spoke for might be small, but it was loud. Loud enough that he had been on the platform with Messenger this morning. He could have provided some insight for the story. But, now I had a different agenda.

Duffet's group was extreme. He might well know something about a murder committed just for the hate of it. I'd met plenty of sincere and compassionate people who wanted to reform immigration policy. Duffet wasn't one of them. Duffet and his group were likely to see the murder of any illegal immigrant as one less chance to contaminate the gene pool. If this girl was murdered just for being Latina, even if he wasn't responsible, he might have some idea of who was. It was time to push harder for that interview.

But Duffet had no interest in meeting with me. He liked talking to the faithful. He had no time for the merely inquisitive. Well, Skye was my plan for getting past his defenses. Skye is a blond-haired, blue-eyed senior at North High, with the guileless charm of a 4-year-old. And, I figured, he was the perfect bait for a zealot out to convert the young to the path of racial purity.

I sat beside Skye prompting him while he called Duffet's office.

An appointment at Coloradoans for Immigration Reform was surprisingly easy to arrange. They would be happy to interview with a young man looking to learn more about the organization. Of course, they couldn't guarantee that Skye could meet with Mr. Duffet, who was a terribly busy man. But Mr. Duffet was in the office, and with Skye so anxious to meet him, well, probably a brief introduction could be arranged. Skye breezed through the phone call. He wanted to learn all about their organization, he was fascinated to meet Duffet. Skye wasn't lying. He is interested in everything from chaos theory to the politics of ancient Mesopotamia. And he'd likely find any new acquaintance fascinating. Still, sometimes I also worry about my influence on him.

With my bait in tow I headed to Duffet's office. It was located in an office building just a couple of blocks from the Capitol, a perfect location for lobbying the state legislature, and not the cheapest digs in Denver. I walked into the glass lobby, Skye bouncing around me like a golden retriever out for a romp.

Lily, the receptionist at Coloradoans for Immigration Reform, was a thin, middle-aged woman dressed for Wall Street. She returned Skye's smile with a firm handshake. Clearly this was a get-down-to-business woman, which meant it took Skye five minutes instead of his usual three to completely win her over. Skye just brings out the mother in women. Well, except for me. I'm not sure there is any mother in me.

Lily showed us around the office. She pointed out pictures of Duffet with local and national dignitaries, including one group photo with his face wedged next to a former Vice President, like a kid trying to steal a place in someone else's family portrait. We saw plaques and awards and we each received a signed copy of Duffet's manifesto for immigration reform. Lily handed mine over reluctantly. Clearly I was just gatecrashing this party.

Finally, Lily led us down the hall, explaining she had arranged for Skye to meet with the volunteer coordinator.

"His office is right around the corner. He has a brief film I know you'll enjoy." She smiled to Skye.

That was my cue. Lily didn't even notice that I was left behind as she walked off chattering.

I held back until Skye and Lily rounded the corner. Someplace in the tour we had passed Duffet's office. It wasn't hard to locate again. Just look for the big corner office away from the bustling activity.

I leaned nonchalantly against his door, listening for voices. Nothing. That was good. I didn't want to walk in on a meeting where I might be recognized, or get thrown out before I even had a chance to give someone a good reason to toss me.

I knocked once and stepped in. Duffet was seated behind a large cherry desk, hunched over a stack of papers he studied intently.

"Just a minute, Natalie," he said, holding up a hand, palm out, without looking up.

"Mr. Duffet, my name is Jo, Jo Walker," I said, walking up and grabbing his hand with a solid shake.

He looked up, pulling his hand back quickly.

"Who did you say you are?" he demanded.

"Jo," I said, reaching my hand out again.

Tentatively he took my hand and shook it. A smile moved half way up his face while his eyes sharpened with suspicion.

Clearly he had no idea who I was. He couldn't decide if I was a friend or foe. From what I knew of the man, that was the way he saw the world, friend or foe, no middle ground there.

"Did we have an appointment, ah, Mrs. Walker?"

"Well, no. I've been trying to speak with you for several days and stopped by the office hoping I could catch you in. There wasn't anyone at the front desk, so I came on back." No need to mention that I had arranged for the front desk desertion.

"I heard you speak at the rally this morning," I added with what I hoped was an ingratiating smile.

At the mention of the rally, his posture relaxed. He was moving onto firmer ground. Here was an admirer, one of the flock.

"Well, it's a pleasure to meet you, Jo. But I am so sorry, I'm afraid I don't have much time. Let me call someone who can help you."

My hand covered the phone receiver a split second before his reached it.

"Really, Mr. Duffet, I would appreciate just a few minutes of your time. I only have a few questions."

His smile faded, but he leaned back and spread his hands. "Well, of course if we can keep this to a few minutes. What was it you wanted to ask?"

I pulled a side chair up to his desk and took a seat directly across from him. Being right in his face would give me a better chance to see lies if they surfaced. And, I wasn't interested in making the man comfortable. If he were a bit on edge, well, you never know what might pop out unrehearsed.

I lobbed him a couple of soft questions. What was his position on illegal immigration? How did he propose dealing with illegal immigrants who had been in the country for years, who had family here? Did he support an amnesty program? How about temporary work permits?

It wasn't as if I didn't already know the answers. They rolled out of his mouth like scripted lines. Time to move closer to the bone.

I pulled out one of the many brochures Lily had peppered us with, this one titled *A Call to Action*.

"I see from your brochure that you encourage your members to take action to stop illegal immigration. Do you have any particular actions in mind?"

Still feeling he was on comfortable ground, Duffet recited, "We encourage them to participate in border patrols in Texas and Arizona, to call the police if they have information about illegals in their neighborhoods, not to hire illegals or buy from companies who do."

I smiled serenely.

"You don't ever suggest they might want to take it a step further?"

Duffet sat forward in his chair, the suspicion returning to his eyes.

"I don't know what you mean."

"A couple of weeks ago several members of your organization were cited by the police for vandalism and harassment of local Latinos. Do you support their actions? Do you think some of your members might feel justified in a little more extreme extra-legal harassment? How far do you think your members might go to encourage people to move on back where they came from?"

I tried to sound disinterested, objective, just asking, no threat here. But, I never had mastered the art of duplicity. And Duffet wasn't fooled. Suspicion turned to anger.

"We never encourage illegal activities. What action our members take is their business, not ours. And I'd like to know why it is yours. Who exactly are you?"

I elected not to answer his question.

"Tell me, Mr. Duffet, what do you know about the young Latina woman who was murdered Saturday night?"

Duffet stood abruptly, slamming his hands on his desk.

"So, that's what this is about. Are you with the press? I never agreed to an interview with the press. You'll have to leave."

I stood but still faced him.

"Interesting that you haven't denied knowing about the murder, Mr. Duffet. Just what is your involvement? Did one of your members get a bit carried away? Or, maybe you don't think he went too far after all."

Duffet grabbed the phone and dialed.

"Fred, get building security up here, now." He glared at me. "What newspaper are you with? I'll have you in court for illegal entry."

"Better get your story straight before you try that, Duffet. I was invited here." I started to the door, but turned to face him. "You can get me thrown out, Duffet, but you still haven't answered my question. You really don't want to see that headline: Jim Duffet Refuses to Comment on Death of Murdered Girl."

Security pushed into the office, two men the size of refrigerators. Duffet held up a hand to stop them. He still hadn't figured out who I was, or if I could deliver on that threat. But he wasn't ready to take the chance.

Barely holding back his anger, he hissed, "I've got nothing to gain by murdering some whoring bitch. You want to find out what happened to that girl, you go talk to Carlos Rivera. He smuggles them over the border. He's the one who's got something to hide. Now get out of here."

He signaled to the two security guys. They took their positions, one on each side. Where did they find these guys? Weren't there better job opportunities for linebackers who couldn't make it in the NFL?

They walked me first out of the office and then out of the building. I was beginning to wonder what I could serve them for dinner if they escorted me home. Slabs of beef, no doubt.

But they left me standing on the street corner.

Now what? I thought about going back for Skye, but didn't figure I had much chance of getting back into the building. Besides, I couldn't imagine Lily letting any harm come to him. She was probably serving him ice cream in the lunch room by now, along with a lecture on the dangers of making the wrong kinds of friends. Well, she wasn't entirely wrong on that count.

I decided to give it 15 minutes. I sat on a concrete stoop in front of the building and waited, thinking about the interview.

Duffet was no saint, that's for sure. But I've interviewed hundreds of people . . . guilty, innocent, and indifferent. I can usually tell when someone is lying or hiding information. And Duffet didn't seem to be doing either. He might not mourn the girl's death. In fact, he might approve of it. But he wasn't involved. And if his members were, he didn't know about it.

But, what had he meant by implicating Carlos Rivera? Rivera was a prominent Denver businessman and politician. Could he honestly be involved in smuggling illegal immigrants into Colorado? What a scandal that would be. Or, was that a red herring

Duffet tossed out to misdirect me? I'd need to take a closer look into that.

It was only another 5 minutes before Skye walked out of the office building. He was wearing a broad smile and carried a bag of popcorn in one hand and a can of Coke in the other. I guess the lunchroom was out of ice cream. I commandeered his soda and headed back toward the car. I figured I had done as much to earn a treat as he had. Skye just smiled and offered me some of his popcorn.

Well, if Duffet wasn't going to provide a lead, then once more unto the breach. I'd have to find someone who could.

Chapter Four

When we walked back in the office Ed was standing at the coffee machine filling his mug with sludge that looked like it had been cooking since daybreak. Ed is not a Starbucks man. If it is brown and has enough caffeine to wake the comatose, that is his kind of brew.

"Hey boss," I said, "Utopia been nuked yet?"

His scowl would have flattened a stand of pines.

"That's not funny, Jo."

I kind of thought it was, and Skye risked a small smile, but Ed isn't known for having a sense of humor even on his good days.

"Yeah, well you didn't spend your morning listening to the approach of Armageddon in the streets of Denver. Got a few minutes for me and my star pupil?"

"Just leave Utopia out of it. What can I do for you?"

As we walked to Ed's office I told him about our visit to Duffet and the all-illegal-immigrants-should-be-wrapped-in-burlap-sacks-and-thrown-back-in-the-Rio-Grande crowd.

"Skye got popcorn. I got nothing. Duffet suggested that I talk to Carlos Rivera though. He said Rivera is smuggling illegals into Denver. At least that's what he implied. What's your take?"

Ed may not like the way the world turns, but he keeps an eagle eye on it. Rivera was a force in Denver politics. Once a Colorado State Senator, and now a Denver City Councilman and adviser to the mayor. If Rivera was less than squeaky clean, there was a good chance Ed would have heard.

We had reached Ed's office. He walked around his desk and sat facing us, his fingers drumming the calendar that covered his desk.

"Honestly, Jo, I haven't heard anything like that." He paused. "But I guess I wouldn't be surprised either. Rivera's family has been in Denver for generations. He's got strong ties to the entire Latino community. He's been making friends, and enemies too, with his strident insistence on immigrant rights. I've dismissed it as partisan rhetoric. But it may go deeper. He's carrying around a lot of resentment. I don't know where he came by all that anger, but I believe he'd smuggle people into the country just to stick it to people like Duffet." Another pause.

"I'll make a few calls, see what I can find out. I'll get back to you, but probably not until tomorrow."

I would have to be satisfied with that. It was getting late anyhow, and I had promised Skye I'd take him home for dinner with the family, his reward for playing nice with Duffet's folks.

Leaving Ed to marshal his sources, we headed back to my office for a couple of quick phone calls to arrange family dinner plans. I knew Skye would always be welcome, but I added another diner less likely to receive a warm welcome.

I looked over at Skye sitting quietly beside me.

Well, he wanted to be a reporter. Who knew where he might end up ... Afghanistan, Syria? Dinner at my house could be a good primer on embedded warfare.

To lighten the blow, I threw him the keys to my 4Runner.

"Here, you can drive us home." His face lit up like a beacon. He was sprinting toward the car while I was still rising from my seat. Enthusiasm ... the boy had no lack of enthusiasm.

Home is the house I share with my BGF Linda, her 16-year-old daughter Jessie, their Border Collie Bosco, and my midnight-black cat, Zephyr. "BGF" (Best Girl Friend) is the term that Jessie uses to describe my relationship with Linda. Our friendship started in high school when I arrived in Boulder from Berkeley, bruised and angry after the death of my mother. It is an unlikely friendship. At 43, I'm still trying to figure out what I want to be when I grow up. Linda had her life planned by the time she was 12. She'd decided on a career in law, where she wanted to go to school, where she wanted to live, how many kids she wanted to have. Her life plan was written, and she had been pretty much on course. Then her husband, Larry, was killed in a car accident.

It wasn't long after the accident that I came back to Denver from Boston. I moved in. Linda couldn't make herself leave the home she and Larry shared, but she also couldn't quiet the memories of him in every room. She'd hoped I might chase away some of those shadows.

When Skye pulled up to the house, a blue Civic hybrid was just pulling into the driveway ahead of us, political rhetoric plastered across the back bumper. A "Black Lives Matter" flag flying from the antenna. Hazel had arrived. Hazel believes in advertising and acting on her politics. If someone decided to market wind-powered automobiles, Hazel would be whipping around town with a mast sticking out of her sunroof. Hazel was Linda's mother, and the problem I'd invited to dinner.

Linda loves her mother, but she doesn't much like or approve of her. Linda likes the status quo. Or at least that's what she thinks she likes. By the time I showed up in Boulder, Linda had spent the years from diapers to pantyhose being dragged by her mother from one political protest to the next. I'd arrived just as Linda's burnout was creating noxious fumes for the relationship. It never recovered.

For me Hazel was a lifeline. I was furious with my Dad for dragging me away from Berkley. The first few months we spent a lot of time staring at each other over the top of half-empty pizza boxes.

Then Hazel rode to the rescue. My father got a lifetime supply of cream of mushroom soup casseroles. He swears he still has some of them in the bottom of his freezer. I got swept off to demonstrations, sit-ins, consciousness raisings, and vision quests. I licked stamps, stuffed envelopes, handed out fliers, and once even got tear-gassed, though Hazel was horrified and swore to my father she'd never let anything like that happen again. I'm not sure what my father made of the whole thing. We'd been overtaken by a force of nature.

Hazel greeted me as I walked to the door. She looked like someone you would expect to meet hosting a booth at a church bake sale — a sweet smile, hair trimly cut in tight gray curls. Great camouflage. Hazel could outmaneuver, intimidate, and bully true confessions faster than anyone I've ever known. She also had more genuine compassion than anyone I've ever known. A knockout combination.

I walked with Hazel into the kitchen, leaving Skye to rummage for company.

"So, Jo, any particular reason I'm braving my daughter's wrath for dinner?"

"Ed wants me to check out a murder that happened a few nights ago."

"I heard about it."

I didn't even bother asking Hazel how she knew. She has a network of friends that makes the CIA look like amateurs. A cross between the Baker Street irregulars and the Joint Chiefs of Staff, there isn't anything that happens in Denver that they don't know or can't find out about. And they have the political clout to make state politicians pay attention, or at least hide when they come asking questions. The problem is that there is usually some political agenda attached when the information starts flying. I respected these people, but that didn't mean I wanted to be in the line of fire.

"I wanted to see if you have any suggestions."

"Well, what have you found out so far?" Hazel asked.

"Almost nothing, Hazel, I just started today."

"But you went to see Duffet?"

Jeez, information was flying fast here, even for Hazel.

"Yeah, but I didn't learn much. I'd say he's not involved."

Hazel didn't look convinced, or maybe it was just that she thought I'd answered the wrong question.

"If you know something, Hazel, you should tell me."

"I don't know anything, Jo. It's just that there may be more involved than you realize. I want you to be careful."

It took me a moment to digest that last statement.

"How can I be careful if I don't even know what you think might be dangerous?"

"Just be careful, Jo. I know you like to jump into things with both feet. Just slow down on this. Don't push it until you can see the terrain."

This from the woman who'd faced down the National Guard, and spent weeks in jail for pushing at every institution that crossed her. Where was this warning coming from? Maybe more important, who was I being warned against? Hazel wouldn't say more. She swept off to the dining room in search of her granddaughter.

Dinner was uneventful. My conversation with Hazel had set me on edge or I might have enjoyed the spectacle of teenage melodrama.

Jessie's best friend, Jill, was part of the dinner crowd. Jessie and Jill are inseparable. If you call one, both show up. But Skye had eyes for only one of the duo. No matter how he tried for the cool, senior stance, he just couldn't help oozing on Jessie. I trusted Skye. Still, Jessie was a ditsy sophomore, a kid. Skye was a senior, a man about to go out in the world.

Luckily, as I saw it, Jessie showed no interest. In fact, she showed no interest in dating boys at all. While her girlfriends fretted and schemed, Jessie blithely went her way as if boys were no more interesting than last year's fashion.

Linda worried, but I figured Jessie just needed time. And if she didn't start dating until she graduated from college that suited me fine.

Jill didn't share Jessie's indifference to Skye. She bought the cool, senior thing hook, line, and sinker. Jill's dinner consisted of long, furtive looks at Skye, nervous giggles at his every glance, and quiet wistful sighs punctuated by three bites of salad.

I watched the activities at the dinner table with a detachment I wouldn't have thought possible a few hours ago when I was so fondly appreciating my "family." Whatever Hazel had meant to convey with her warning, what I felt was angry. And maybe just a tad afraid.

Chapter Five

After dinner, Jessie and Jill disappeared into the realm of teenage intrigue, sequestered behind the closed door of Jessie's bedroom. Linda disappeared into the study, briefcase in hand, ready for another long night of legal maneuvering. Skye and Hazel disappeared into the night in search of adventure in the blue Civic. Now there was a pair that would bear watching.

All that charm and blatant innocence masked a truly impressive potential for civil disruption. After watching Skye in action at Duffet's office, I had a new respect for his power. Hazel of course was Hazel, indomitable and with more energy than a room full of two-year-olds. If Hazel decided to take Skye under her wing the way she had me, I was going to have some explaining to do to Skye's parents.

But my conscience just wasn't up to dragging myself back out in the car to take Skye home myself. I'd survived Hazel's influence; I suppose Skye would too.

My plan for the evening was to curl up with some good reading and plot my investigation into Duffet's organization.

After an hour on the sofa with Duffet's manifesto and all the other propaganda Skye and I had collected, I decided there was no good reading to be had there. I have my own prejudices. If you're going to insist that English be the only language in the country, I figure the least you can do is use it well. How about a little imagination? All Duffet seemed able to accomplish was a tired litany of old complaints and stereotypes. By the time I had finished reading I wanted to keep all the immigrants here and send Duffet and his entire organization to Mexico. Maybe he could make new friends at a drug cartel.

I decided to call it quits, resigning myself to a night filled with nightmares of armed men chasing each other through clusters of organ pipe cactus. Duffet would like that. It had a kind of John Wayne feel to it.

It wasn't dreams of Duffet, though, that woke me in a cold sweat in the early morning. Gail Bachman lay in a pool of red. Her once tense body relaxed in a way it had never been when she was alive. Her chocolate eyes staring at me in accusation. It was a nightmare I feared would haunt me for the rest of my life.

Gail was a whistle blower. She met with me, her trim black hair bouncing with her staccato walk, bringing the evidence that would expose her company for bribing Boston city officials for contracts. Later, Gail pacing with anxiety, her arms wrapped tightly around herself. She wanted out. She was afraid. I pushed. I played on her conscience. I condemned the cheating, worried over the risk of shoddy work. She was the only one who could expose these thieves. I offered reassurances. I discounted her fears.

Then a phone call. She insisted we meet — 7:00 p.m. at the Hatch Shell on the Esplanade. She didn't show. Exhausted from searching half the night for her, I returned home to find the police waiting on my apartment doorstep.

There had been a break-in, a neighbor told me.

A detective tried to grab me as I ran up the stairs and into my bedroom.

That's where I found Gail. She was sprawled on my bed, her hair now red with blood. Her eyes closed, though in my dream they are open, always open, staring at me.

I blamed myself. I still do. A woman was dead and I was as culpable as the killers. I had forced their hand and this was their answer. I finished the story. City officials lost their jobs, her company paid large fines. But the murder was never solved.

I was on my way home to Colorado within a month. When Ed called with a job offer, I accepted. I could stay in the newspaper business but keep out of the rough and tumble world of hard news.

Or, that had been my plan. Now, here was another murder. I couldn't run from this one. If I started running again, where would it stop? I suppose that was Ed's point. But I didn't like it.

Chapter Six

One night was all I planned to give to the horrors of the past. I lay in bed waiting for the sun to rise and warm my heartache. Duffet didn't seem to know anything. It was time to look elsewhere. When I pulled myself from bed, my first call was to Councilman Rivera.

From everything I knew about Rivera, I didn't expect to like him. It's not that I dislike politicians. Politicians are my bread and butter. A news reporter without politicians is like a foxhound without a fox. What's the point?

But Rivera was a man with a chip on his shoulder. His protests were too strident. He cared more about the fight than the casualties. I'd seen too many crusaders who left bodies strewn across the political spectrum. In that way, he was more like Duffet than either one of them would have liked to think — two sides of the same issue, both more concerned with being right than with the people they might hurt.

On the bright side, Rivera was a Democrat and would expect a reporter from *The Review* to be in his corner. I wouldn't need to bring Skye to get past the reception desk.

At 10:00 a.m. I walked into his office dressed in a navy blue suit that I thought seemed vaguely reminiscent of a Catholic school uniform, minus the pleats. Maybe I could evoke a few pleasant memories, put him off his guard.

Rivera stood and walked from behind his desk to greet me

with a handshake. He was gray-haired and clean-shaven with a wide smile. His handshake was strong. He was either enthusiastic about the interview, or he was claiming his place as dominant male. I didn't know which yet.

Rivera had already launched into his canned speech about the rights of immigrants. He thought he had my number . . . a liberal journalist looking to expose the evils of prejudice against Latinos. He was into his standard meet and greet campaign-stop mode. Say a few words to the press, fan the flames of discontent, move on to something important. He didn't notice that I wasn't paying attention. I was staring at the other man in the room.

I don't think of many men as drop-dead gorgeous, but this guy was. He was fit the way a young animal is fit — sleek, muscular, and loose. But he wasn't that young, and I wasn't staring at his good looks. It was the attitude that was getting to me. He didn't move, not a muscle, not a hair, not a flutter of clothing. He might have been a granite statue placed next to Rivera's desk. But his eyes, his eyes were all threat, threat and scorn. *Cause trouble here, little girl, and I'll make you wish you were never born.*

I've never been good at backing off from a challenge, even when I know I should. It's gotten me in trouble since I started walking, and I'm not showing any signs of reform. This was a provocation. Nobody looked at me in that tone of voice. Looking straight into those threatening eyes, I interrupted Rivera.

"I appreciate that you agreed to see me for this interview Councilman, but could you ask your Rottweiler to wait outside?"

Rivera's cheerful facade cracked like a sheet of glass.

"Jose, please leave us," he said tersely, and the man left. When his smile returned it barely lifted the corners of his mouth.

"As I was saying, yesterday's rally was just one more attempt to keep the Latinos in Colorado from getting the respect and privilege they deserve as valuable members of this community. It's time for the governor to take a stand against these people."

I stared at him blankly. Murder had driven the rally completely from my mind.

"Councilman, I didn't request this interview to discuss the rally. I'd like you to comment on the murder Monday night of the Latina girl found by the Platte River."

I watched him carefully, looking for any sign of fear, any indication that my interest bothered him. I saw none.

"I'm a politician, Ms. Walker, not a policeman. The death of any of my people is a loss to me. But, I don't know anything about this girl, so I can hardly comment until the police have uncovered more information."

"So, you never met this girl?"

"From what I understand, the police haven't even identified her yet."

"I went to see Jim Duffet yesterday. He suggested you might have some information about how the girl got into this country."

Rivera looked at me with a glare that was a match for that of his henchman.

"Duffet is the last man who would have any idea about what I might know."

"Maybe. But he's not the only person who's suggested that you might be helping smuggle illegal immigrants into Denver."

Rivera puffed up like a blowfish.

"Smuggle illegal immigrants into Denver? Tell me Ms. Walker," he made my name sound like a curse, "how long have you lived in Denver? My people lived in the southwest when it still belonged to Spain. My family lived in Colorado when it was still a territory. When the Easterners poured in looking for gold, we were already here. Yet men like Duffet come around telling me who can live in my home. A home his people stole from us, and from the native people. They label my people vagrants and troublemakers. They make our children learn their language. They scatter crumbs for them to live in poverty, doing jobs no one else wants. Don't talk to me about smuggling people illegally into your country."

As he spoke, Rivera got louder and began walking around the office in fits and starts. But I was having a problem with his righteous indignation. The scene felt staged—a little dramatic diatribe to make the bleeding-heart liberal back down, apologize for causing offense. Well, he had the wrong gal for that scenario. I don't like being manipulated and I don't respond well to it. He might as well be handing me an engraved invitation to start digging around in his dirty laundry.

What exactly was Rivera covering up with the bravado and indignation? He didn't seem concerned with squashing rumors that he was smuggling people into the country. In fact, he seemed proud of the idea, whether it was true or not. Like Ed said, he'd do it just to stick it to the other guys. What then?

I doubted I was going to find out anything here. One thing I could say for Duffet, he was proud to say exactly what he thought, no matter how bigoted. Rivera was better skilled at duplicity. This was a man I could interview till doomsday and still have no idea what he actually thought. I had better uses for my time. At his first full pause I stood up, thanked him for his time and walked out the door, leaving him glaring at my back.

Chapter Seven

When I got back to *The Review*, Ed was still locked in his office. I wanted to talk with him about my interview with Rivera, find out if he had been able to get any new information about Rivera's smuggling activities. But Ed rarely closed his office door. When he did, it meant "Do Not Disturb" unless the building was on fire.

Well, I wasn't going to get anywhere waiting for Ed or asking questions of the suspects or their gurus. It was time for News Reporting 101. Get on the phone, pound the pavement, dig in the archives. As long as I was in the office, the archives seemed like a good place to start.

We had enough back copy on Rivera to write a biography. Two biographies. The first of the community leader, a family man, a civil servant dedicated to the welfare of Denver and all its citizens, but with a special place in his heart for the people of his ancestral home. The second: a biography of a petty tyrant, well skilled in the arts of political horse trading and arm twisting.

The information on Duffet was just as profuse, and just as two-sided. A good man fighting a just cause, or a self-serving opportunist hitched to the current hot issue.

All that was missing was any real information about what these men did when they weren't standing in the public spotlight. Was Duffet a man who would condone or even encourage murder? Even if Rivera did aid illegal immigrants, what could he possibly gain from the death of this young woman? I wasn't finding the answers to those questions in old newspapers.

In fact, what did I know about this murder? Just that the woman was murdered and she was Latina. Maybe the murder was racially motivated, maybe not. I didn't even know who the woman was, what she looked like, how old she was, where she was from. Did the police have answers to those questions? Or was this just a body without a home, name, and life? It seemed impossible.

People couldn't disappear without anyone noticing. Of course, I knew they did. And young women on city streets did. But this was murder. I couldn't make sense of it. Murdering a young woman wasn't going to make all the Latinos in Denver pack up and move back to where they came from. Some people might be angry when all the facts came out. But we're not talking armed rebellion.

Criminals don't always make sense. I had to stop trying to think my way into an explanation. I needed to get my teeth into this story. I decided to rev up my courage and make the trip I didn't want to make . . . a visit to the crime scene. I collected my research papers and headed to the river.

I've always disliked being places where violent crimes had been committed. But since Boston it's become worse . . . buried images pushing to the surface, guilt and horror clamoring for my attention. Still, I had to try. How could I hope to find the heart of the story if I couldn't face its basic tragedy? A young woman was dead. All the politics of men like Duffet and Rivera didn't amount to a hill of beans in the face of that single loss.

Outside it was cold and gray, weather we sometimes see in Denver in the winter, but rare this late in the spring. I parked on the 15th Street overpass that spanned the South Platte. The crime scene was just blocks from Denver Skate Park.

The chill weather hadn't dampened the enthusiasm of the young skateboarders. Their yells penetrated the gray like flashes of color. I wondered if they even knew what had happened so close to their turf. Would it mean anything to them, or just seem like a scene from a TV crime show?

I climbed down the embankment, grabbing tufts of brown grass to slow my descent to the bike path. The South Platte River was dark, its currents masked by the matte finish.

I walked along the path. I don't know what I had expected. Maybe some bright yellow crime scene tape. Or, bundles of flowers and teddy bears like the monuments of mementos constructed by mourners of well-loved children or well-known celebrities.

There were few markers here. Skid marks gouged in the grass where men had struggled to gain a foothold on the muddy slope as they lifted the body up the hill. Light patches on the concrete wall where graffiti had been painted over with mismatched paint.

What I had expected or hoped to find here was long gone. There was no feel of the girl, or the person who had killed her. There was no psychic residue. The crime scene was as dead as the girl who had been left here.

Still I sat on the river bank, half concealed by the brittle tall weeds. I looked into the dark water. Something awful had happened here. Not the murder itself. But a young woman was killed and her body left in this place, disfigured perhaps to hide her identity. Were her parents searching frantically for her? Did her friends miss her? Or, had she been so alone that there was no one who would know she was gone? Someone owed her at least that, to know who she was, and why someone held her life in such small regard that they would wipe her away as if she had never existed.

The violence of the murder was frightening, but it was the loss that angered me.

It reminded me of the silence my mother's death had left in my home. But it was more than that. I was angered by the greed, the stealing of the thing that was most precious of all that a person had: their life, their impact on the lives of others, their place in the world. The police were investigating. But they were committed to keeping emotions restrained. Would they be willing to rattle the high-profile cages necessary to shake loose a lead? Would they be willing to risk the upheaval of escalating racial tensions for the sake of one nameless girl? I didn't know. But I wasn't willing to risk it. I don't distrust the police. Generally I think of them as the good guys. Still, I didn't know if they would hear the silence the way I did.

Well, I wasn't going to let this girl's life end like a pile of garden refuse tossed on the banks of this river. Something had changed for me. I told Ed I would gather enough evidence to prove this wasn't a random street crime ... that it was a hate crime.

But that wasn't enough anymore. I wanted to know who had done this thing. If I could, I would see that her life had meaning. If she couldn't have the promise of her life, at least she could have this: her death would remove one piece of evil from this city. It was a rotten bargain, but it was all I had to offer. God, I just wished I knew her name, some small piece of her to hang on to.

I left the crime scene, walking back along the river path, thinking. Someone had to know something about this crime. I thought of Russ. Maybe this murder was his real reason for being at the anti-immigration rally yesterday. He might be on the same hunt I was. But, Russ didn't seem a likely candidate to help me out with this. He would want the story for his own. And even if he was willing to share, the police wanted this tamped down. He wasn't going to risk angering them for me.

So that left Hazel. It wasn't likely she'd been talking with the police. So, she must have another contact. Hazel might be a tough nut to crack, but I knew her weak spot. She could no more let this girl's death go unanswered than she could pour toxic waste in a river, or simply stop recycling for that matter. She just isn't wired to ignore her conscience. My next stop would be Hazel's house.

I left the path and began my climb up the river bank, headed for the overpass where I'd left my car. Through the tall dried grasses I could just make out my car beside the road. Something was wrong. The passenger side door was open. As I drew closer I saw a man rummaging through the papers I'd left on the seat. I yelled out and started scrambling up the hill. But the muddy slope slowed me. The man glanced up. I had a clear view of his face — dark, squat features that appeared too big for his face, curling black hair that rested on his collar, probably Latino. He saw my stumbling approach, and smiled at me, a look that was half leer and half smirk. Clearly he wasn't concerned that I could identify him. He grabbed a handful of papers, and darted out of the car. He ran down the street to a parked black SUV and was gone before I reached the pavement.

The passenger-side window of my car was smashed. My research papers about Rivera and Duffet were gone. And the jerk had urinated on the floor mats.

I couldn't figure out the motive. The research wasn't anything secret. I could just dig it up again with a few hours work. Maybe it was an attempt to intimidate me. But by whom? And why? It wasn't like I knew anything. Duffet didn't seem like a good candidate. I couldn't imagine him with Latino cohorts. That left Rivera. But what could Rivera gain by this petty vandalism? Maybe he wanted to see if I was drafting a giant expose, as if? Or, maybe it was someone I hadn't even thought of yet.

I wouldn't be that easily put off. I brushed the glass off the driver's side of the car and drove to my local gas station, windows open to disperse the reek. The guys at the station knew my car and had worked on it before. But they weren't thrilled at the condition I delivered it in this time. Still they took it in hand and gave me an old VW beetle as a loaner. I headed to Hazel's, limping along the road in a cloud of exhaust.

Hazel lived in a trendy section of Denver where the small 1940s bungalows were being snapped up and scraped away, replaced by looming McMansions. Hazel's house had lost both adjoining neighbors to the giants. Now it stood as a place of composure and restraint braced against the encroaching symbols of wealth and prestige. It was such a caricature of the woman herself it could only be cosmic irony. Like much else, Hazel didn't take the symbolism seriously. She likes her neighbors, and if they are frivolous in their spending, it is none of her concern.

Hazel was in her garden with Skye. Why was I not surprised? It was late enough in the afternoon for Skye to be out of school. Hazel had clearly recruited him for some garden project. They were both swathed in coils of garden hose.

"Oh good, Jo, just the person we need. Take this end," she said, handing me the hose end, "and go hold it by the spigot over there. Skye and I are just plotting the course for the drip irrigation for the flowers."

"Hazel, I wanted to talk with you about last night." I just wasn't sure I wanted to do it with Skye listening. I was already feeling guilty about hooking him up with Hazel. I didn't want him involved any further in this investigation.

"Fine, just do it while you're holding the end. Stand by the spigot. Now go on."

"Hazel, I can hardly hold a conversation while standing across the yard." This was not a conversation I wanted to share with her neighbors either.

When she didn't respond, I picked up the end and stomped toward the spigot like a rebellious 5-year-old. Skye of course was all smiles, huddled with Hazel as they alternately held up different sprinkler heads and plastic gizmos. Well, if shouting was what was required, then shouting it would be.

"Hazel, about last night, how did you know I had gone to see

Duffet?" No answer from the huddle. I dropped the hose and stalked back across the yard.

"Look, Hazel, this is important. The police don't seem to know who the murdered girl was. I was just at the crime scene. Somebody killed that girl and just tossed her aside on the river bank. Maybe it was racial hatred, maybe something else. I don't know. But you seem to know something, certainly more than I do."

"I can't tell you, Jo, not now. Annie McIntyre told me you had gone to see Duffet. I suppose Ed told her. Some married couples do still talk once in a while. But it was another friend who told me that there might be more going on with the death than was obvious. He thought I should warn you to be careful. He was concerned. But it was said in confidence. You're not the only person he wants to protect. That's all I can tell you. I can't betray that confidence. I will ask if he'd be willing to talk to you, but that's the best I can do."

I knew I had to accept that.

"Do you really need my help here?" I asked, looking at the spigot.

"No," she said. "Skye and I can handle it."

"Well, I'm going home then. Thanks, Hazel. I'd appreciate anything you can do."

I gave Skye a smile and headed to my limping transport.

Chapter Eight

I drove home from Hazel's feeling blue in a way I hadn't anticipated. After visiting the crime scene I had expected to feel loss, grief, even guilt. But I hadn't felt anything except anger. It was as if the girl hadn't died, she had simply evaporated and taken most of my feelings with her. No face, no name, and so, no person. I had to learn more about this young woman before she vanished from all our minds along with the crime against her. Tomorrow I would find someone who knew her. For tonight all I wanted was a quiet night on the deck with a good book and a tall glass of sangria.

That thought vanished quickly as I pulled into the driveway. Linda was half visible kneeling in the dirt under the lilac bush. She was dressed for court in a gray suit. But, she was digging frantically with a hand shovel, staring furtively around the bush at our neighbor Bill. Her odd behavior jarred me right out of my melancholy. I have to say this about my family, it's hard to stay down when they're around; they are just too entertaining.

Bill was new to the neighborhood, and as far as I was concerned, every time he walked out the door property values improved. He was working in his yard putting a final buff on his Harley. Despite the cold, he was stripped to the waist and his muscles glistened with the same deep shine as his bike. Yum for both.

Linda, on the other hand, looked a wreck. She had torn off her suit jacket. Brown rings of sweat mixed with dirt were spreading under the arms of her white silk blouse. Her stockings were ripped and her heels were caked with mud. This was not Linda's usual gardening outfit.

I wasn't even out of the car before she greeted me with hushing gestures and grimaces. As far as I could tell, Linda was crouched behind the lilac to hide from Bill. I figured it was worth the walk to saunter over and find out why.

When I got within reach Linda pulled me down beside her. "Do you have to be so obvious?"

"Obvious about what? I didn't know we were running clandestine operations in the backyard this week. Did Hazel beat me back here?" Hazel was the obvious choice as leader of clandestine or bizarre behavior.

She smashed her hand over my mouth and whispered, "Just be quiet and don't call attention to yourself."

Like no one would find it suspicious that she was gagging me behind a lilac bush.

"Linda, why are you hiding from Bill?"

"I'm not hiding. I just don't want to talk with him right now."

"Oh, well that's different. Why not?"

Linda fell back against the bush, dropped her hands into her lap, and frowned. "Oh, for Christ's sake, he's a plumber."

"A plumber?" I'd never found that sufficient reason to avoid someone. Besides, Bill wasn't exactly a plumber. His family owned one of the biggest plumbing companies in Denver.

"He runs the family business, Linda. I think he has an MBA from CU."

"That's not the point. He's 53 years old. I could be his daughter."

Yeah, right, if he started fathering children when he was 10.

"And look at that thing he drives around."

I loved to look at that thing he drove around. Sleek, black, lustrous. Just looking at it gave me the tingles.

"He's a 53-year-old plumber with a Harley. He's got tattoos. He drinks Coors at biker bars with his friends Bubba and Big Hank. God, he probably votes Republican."

"So do you."

Linda glared at me. "That's different and you know it."

Linda is more likely to find fault with people who agree with her than those who don't. She gets this odd split from her parents. Linda's father was a lawyer from a family that had been laying down the law since Colorado became a state. He believed in decorum, in the rule of rules, and held the bootstrap theory of life. Hard work was the road to success, welfare was for the morally weak, and government should keep its nose out of his affairs. On the other hand, Linda's mother was a rabble-rouser and firebrand. She had been arrested three times for trespassing and civil disobedience. She framed her arrest papers and hung them beside the family portraits that lined the walls of their home. Generations of disapproving men glared at the evidence that this misguided woman had somehow invaded their bloodline.

Linda followed in her father's footsteps, but her mother's voice sometimes popped out of her mouth like an unexpected guest. It's not surprising Linda has difficulty sorting the good guys from the bad. I just couldn't figure why she was so sure Bill was one of the bad guys.

"Well Linda, Jessie likes him and she's hardly what you'd call easy to please."

"I could make Jessie decide she likes her worst enemy after all just by giving them the cold shoulder. It's a mother thing."

"I give up. Whatever is bothering you, decide what to do so I can go have my dinner."

Linda poked her head around the lilac bush again and gave

Bill an annoyed look. "Is he going to spend the rest of the day polishing that thing? Why couldn't a nice family move in next door? Someone with nice kids, maybe a golden retriever, not Mad Max and his road machine."

"Linda, I've only talked with Bill a few times, but he seems like a nice guy."

"Maybe, but women like me do not fall for guys like him."

"You're falling for Bill?"

"No, I'm just saying that I wouldn't."

Linda hadn't been interested in a man since her husband died. This could be great news. But Linda looked terrified. Best to let her work this out in her own time.

I peered around the bush. "Well, we have to do something. He's walking over here."

With a groan Linda scrunched further behind the bush.

"Okay, here's the plan," I said. "I'll run over, jump on the Harley and take off down the back alley. When he comes after me, you make a dash for the house." This was purely a self-serving scheme to get me on that bike. I was half standing before Linda pulled me back down.

"Get real, Jo, we don't need to do anything that childish."

Oh, right, like playing hide and seek under the lilac bush.

"Well, we're just going to have to stand up and face the man unless you want to crawl for cover."

Bill had thrown his rag to the side and was walking in our direction. As I stood he smiled warmly and gave a nod. With a smile like that he could be 103 years old with Neanderthal friends named Grog and Urg. I wouldn't mind a bit.

I turned to give Linda a nudge only to see her scurrying on all fours through the raspberry bushes. Ouch, that had to hurt.

"Hi. Bill, how's it going?"

"Good, you?"

"Not bad."

"I thought I heard Linda over here. I just wanted to tell her that I'm having friends over for a backyard barbecue next Saturday. I'd like you both to come, and bring Jessie too."

From the corner of my eye I could just see Linda rounding the rhubarb and heading into the garage, still on all fours.

"That sounds great, Bill. I'd love to. I'm sure Linda's around here somewhere," I said, staring at the now vacant garage door. "I'll be sure to pass on the invitation."

Bill looked confused for a minute.

"Okay. There's something else. I saw a guy hanging around your place this afternoon. He was parked across the street in a black SUV. When I went over to check him out, he took off."

"What time was that?"

"Couple of hours ago."

"Can you describe him?"

"Nothing too specific, short, stocky. Probably Latino. Hard to tell in the car."

That sounded too much like the man who had trashed my car. Maybe he had decided to stop by the house to see if I'd come home, looking to cause more trouble. It chilled me to think of him hanging out around the house.

Bill continued looking at me.

"Is there some kind of trouble here, Jo?"

"I don't know, Bill. Just some people who aren't very happy about a story I'm writing. Probably nothing to worry about. Still, I don't like it."

"Well if you need anything, you let me know. I can have some of my friends drive by and check out the place occasionally."

"Friends?"

He gave me that same clueless look Jessie had perfected for her mother.

"Just some guys I hang out with," he said looking over at the Harley.

"Thanks Bill, I really don't think that's necessary."

Great, I thought as I turned back to the house, some people have neighborhood watch programs; I'd just arranged to have the Hell's Angels patrolling the street.

Chapter Nine

Hazel called that night. Her source for information about the killing was a state government social worker who organized an anti-trafficking committee, a guy named Latif Brown. That raised my eyebrows. The anti-trafficking people weren't generally concerned with your run-of-the-mill illegal immigration. They showed up when people were dragged into the country against their will for forced labor or prostitution. Was Carlos Rivera into a darker trade than his good-guy politics proclaimed?

Early the next morning I showed up at the marble-faced state office building where Mr. Brown worked in downtown Denver. Inside the heavy steel doors was a small lobby, carpeted in a sickly, tattered green. Behind a counter at the far wall sat a small but sturdy-looking gray-haired woman. When I explained why I was there, she introduced herself as Marianne Boxer, and told me I was welcome to wait in the lobby until Mr. Brown arrived.

When Latif walked into the reception area, it shrank by half. He was a large man. He wasn't a jolly large man either, no Santa Claus here. He stood erect and taut. And his eyes . . . brilliant green eyes. Where, with all that black hair and black skin, had those green eyes come from? They were the eyes of a mountain lion deciding if this hiker was a likely prospect for lunch. After one look at Latif, if I were a Mexican trafficker, I'd be heading home as quickly as I could, even if it meant running barefoot over the Sonoran desert in

August.

Latif wasn't looking like reporters were his favorite people either. I figured I could either bolt, or put out my hand for a shake and hope he didn't crush it. I opted for the handshake and was surprised by the gentleness of its embrace.

He spoke in a slow, booming voice.

"Hazel tells me you're not so good at taking advice and I had better talk with you myself."

I didn't take the introduction well. I wanted to stalk out the door and go yell at Hazel that it was not okay for her to portray me as a recalcitrant teenager. Simultaneously I wanted to spout apologies like a kid caught stealing flowers from a neighbor's yard. With no good options, I just stared up at the man, sputtering.

After several moments of my almost speaking, Latif turned and walked away. Over his shoulder he called, "My office is this way when you figure out what you're going to say."

I followed him down the narrow hallway. A crowd met me at his office door: a thousand faces. Some were posed shots such as graduations and weddings, others were candid snapshots taken at sports events and other gatherings. Some shocked: battered men behind bars, children hanging on street corners, dressed for the sex trade. Everywhere faces stared at me. Most were women, but many were men. Most were young but not all. Latif's office was a gallery of the victims and survivors he served. It was a room that revealed a man far different from the one I'd met in the reception area. If these were Latif's companions, no wonder the man was so prickly.

I'd been staring at his office for what seemed like five minutes when I crossed gazes with Latif and stopped short.

"I like to remember who I'm working for," he said. "Now, when you're done with the analysis maybe you'd like to ask me what it is that you'd like to know."

I realized with some chagrin that I hadn't yet said a word to the man since meeting him. This was nuts. Time to get professional if I could just collect my thoughts.

"According to Hazel, you think there's something dangerous going on that I need to be careful of. Why?"

"Well, I'd think the dead girl would be your first clue," he said without a hint of irony.

"Yeah, I got that. But what else do you know that makes it so dangerous? What makes you think there's more here than a girl being killed by her boyfriend with some racist graffiti thrown in to confuse the police?"

He walked over and closed the door behind me, making the room feel about the size of a footlocker. He sat behind his desk and indicated a chair for me.

"That girl wasn't just some laborer who paid to get smuggled into the country so she could work here. Sure, she paid to come here, but what happened to her after she arrived wasn't what she paid for or wanted."

"She was trafficked?"

"That's right. She was sixteen years old and they forced her to become a prostitute." He said it without a trace of emotion while looking directly at me. But judging from the pictures around me, I figured there was a whole lot more going on behind that mask.

I didn't know how to keep asking questions without sounding callous. But he wasn't the only one who was angry about the girl's death.

"You knew her?"

"No. I knew about her. Her name was Angela. She was from El Salvador. She'd been in the country less than a year."

"Do you know who she worked for?"

"No. But I would like to find out." This time a bit of the anger leaked out. Even that much wasn't a pretty sight. I was beginning to wonder whether or not Latif was one of the good guys. I had to remind myself that this was a friend of Hazel's. Hazel didn't befriend vigilantes or sociopaths.

"Maybe we could work together, figure out who she worked for, maybe who killed her."

"I don't think so."

"Well, how did you know about her?"

"One of the kids I work with told me about her. They were friends, or at least as much like friends as girls in their predicament can be."

Before I opened my mouth, I knew my request was not going to go over well. "Can I meet her, this friend?"

"Sure," he said with a snap, "as soon as Hell freezes over. I agreed to talk with you so you'd stay out of trouble, not so you'd drag other people into it with you. Now, I've given you fair warning. If you can't listen to sense, then you're on your own."

I liked to decide for myself what sense I listened to. Not only was the story becoming important to me, but I don't like being treated like a child. If I was going to have this man's help, I'd better find a way to get his respect, or at least a bit less of his scorn. Maybe Hazel could explain exactly why she considered this man her friend and help me figure a path through his formidable barricades.

Latif didn't walk me back to the lobby, which was a relief. I was all the way outside again before I felt like there was enough space to breathe.

Chapter Ten

I drove back by Hazel's house on my way to the office. Work on the sprinkler system had progressed. The yards of soaker hose and collection of sprinkler heads had vanished. Water leaked and misted throughout the garden while Hazel bustled through the beds with a measuring stick making adjustments. She turned at my approach.

"Hi, Jo. I was just thinking about you. How'd the meeting with Latif go?"

"That's what I wanted to talk with you about, Hazel. The man was barely civil. I mean, a lot of folks don't like to talk to the press, but this guy was something else. I could barely get him to talk with me at all. What exactly is it about him that you like?"

Hazel frowned at me.

"Well, I don't choose my friends based on their cheerful demeanor. Wouldn't that be tedious? Latif is compassionate, with an abundance of integrity. We've been through some tough battles together, and there are few people I'd rather have at my side. I did have to push him into speaking with you. I think he agreed just because I was so worried. I suppose his heart wasn't in it."

"Well, he didn't tell me much of anything. Can't you give me any more information?"

"I don't have any more. I was just passing on Latif's concern, which, by the way, I take seriously. And I wish you would too. He is no alarmist."

I believed that. It would take a lot to rile that man.

"I would take it seriously if I had any context for understanding it. Can't you do anything?" My voice sounded a tad too much like wheedling, even to my own ear. Hazel frowned at me.

"Jo, I'm trying to get you to be careful, not find allies for your campaign."

"I don't understand, Hazel, you've never walked away from a fight in your life."

"You're swimming in waters I've barely waded through. Latif deals with men whose business it is to intimidate, imprison, and kill people. He wants you to stay away from them. That just seems reasonable. I'm not interested in helping you get closer to them."

I walked over and sat on a bench in the garden beneath a grape trellis. It was still covered with last year's dead leaves that rattled in the background as we spoke.

"Latif told me a little about the girl who was killed. Her name was Angela. I didn't tell you, I went to the crime scene yesterday—the place along the Platte where they found her body. It's just a barren, boot-trampled river bank. There's nothing there, nothing left to indicate a girl was murdered and her body dumped there. It's like she just vanished. The police don't seem to have a clue about who's responsible. Reading between the lines of what Ed has told me, I'm not sure they care. In any case, whatever Latif knows could be the only key. Maybe I do need allies. Angela certainly didn't have any."

"Think about this carefully, Jo. Do you want to get involved in a murder investigation? I'm sure Latif told the police everything he can. Let them handle this. Remember what happened to you in Boston."

"You think I would endanger someone again? You think I learned so little?"

"I'm not talking about what you did. I'm talking about what it did to you. I never blamed you that the woman was murdered. I'm perfectly clear about who pulled the trigger. But you haven't stopped blaming yourself. And there were times when I feared you'd never write again, maybe never work at all. Do you imagine this pursuit won't take you back there? Don't go through this another time. I don't want to go through it again."

Hazel came and sat beside me on the bench. She picked up my hand that sat trembling in my lap and held it tightly.

"Maybe you're right that you have to do this, Jo. Only you know what your conscience dictates. But be prepared. You won't get through it without wrestling some of your own demons."

"I'm not going to be wrestling any demons, Hazel. I'll leave the murder investigating to the police. As soon as I can provide enough evidence to force their investigation. That's what Ed asked for, and that's all I plan to do. Don't worry about me. I've learned my lesson."

"I hope you are just saying that to reassure me, and don't actually believe it. I certainly don't. Just try to go into this with both eyes open and don't let the story sweep you away. And if you need help, don't be too stubborn to ask for it."

"I am asking for it. Help me figure out how to deal with Latif."

"That is not the kind of help I was referring to." Hazel sighed. "Fine, I do have an idea. But you'll need Ed's cooperation and it will take a little work." That did not sound promising. A little work for Hazel could mean anything from a few hours of research to mounting a major campaign. Hazel doesn't see much in life as work. It's all just living your life. It makes her unreliable in estimating the effort needed to accomplish tasks.

"Okay, what's your idea?"

"Latif has been trying to get some public focus on the women who are working and living in Denver brothels. He's partnered with other agencies and interested volunteers to form a citizen's committee on anti-trafficking. They are trying to garner support — individual donors, more funding, and even more consistent enforcement of laws. If you could convince Ed to run a story in *The Review*, it would give the committee some much-needed public visibility and it might just generate enough good will with Latif to give him a reason to help you."

"Sounds like a story Ed would leap on."

"The citizen's committee is meeting tomorrow night. If you can get everything set up with Ed, you could start there."

Now, that did sound like a plan.

"Thanks, Hazel. I'll ask Ed. Will you talk with Latif and set it up for me to go to the meeting? It will probably sound less contrived coming from you."

Hazel smiled.

"It's not like Latif won't know what's going on, Jo. He'll just think the exchange is a good bargain. Or, at least you can hope he will. I'll call him and let you know tonight. Understand, I'll help you because I don't want you alone in this. It doesn't mean I want you to pursue this, or that I think it's a good idea."

"I will be careful, Hazel. I promise."

She drew me to my feet and gave me a bear hug.

"All looks well with the waterworks, how about if I make us some lunch?"

Chapter Eleven

Next evening, with approval from Ed and a nod from Latif, I drove to the state office building where the Colorado Anti-Trafficking Committee was to meet. I didn't know what to expect. Reporters can spend a lot of time sitting through meetings, and it's rarely time well spent. All I needed was a quick story idea, a few leads, and of course Latif's boundless gratitude. Then a quick exit. Well, anything was possible.

I was met at the door by a tall, blond man with Nordic good looks and a broad smile. An attractive man. But he came on too strong with an iron grip handshake and an arm that wrapped around me to lead me towards the battered wooden conference table. His self-assurance put me off, which was odd. I like a man who is confident. But this was too cozy for someone I didn't know. You'd expect someone you just met to be a bit more tentative. Unless of course he was coming on to me, but it seemed like an odd time and place for that.

"You must be Jo Walker from *The Review*. Latif mentioned over coffee this morning that you would be coming to tonight's meeting. I'm the welcoming committee, Mark Miller. I manage the Carlton Hotel downtown."

I knew the place, one of the more upscale downtown hotels, a high rent retreat for the convention center and downtown business visitor.

"Nice place. I've had dinner there a few times. But managing that place sounds like too big a job for one person."

He nodded.

"I say, *I manage the hotel*, but really I do it through my management company, ASP, Incorporated. You're right that it's too much for one person."

"How do you know Latif?"

"He and I go way back. We've been working to get some government action on this prostitution trafficking for some time. It's important to me. The hospitality industry gets a lot of bad press around prostitution, some of it deserved. I want to see an end put to it."

Hm. The right words, but no feeling of conviction. I don't think I'd ever met a man who looked so normal and yet triggered all my alarms quite so quickly.

"Had much success?"

He smiled again.

"Some. It's slow. But we take small steps. Maybe you can add some push to our effort. Let me introduce you around."

I met the rest of the committee, a mix of government employees and private citizens. Together we sat through a depressing four-hour discussion of the growing prostitution network in Denver. Regardless of Mark's tepid claims of progress, it sounded to me as if the battle was losing ground rather than gaining. No wonder Latif was grasping at a straw by wanting a story in *The Review*. I couldn't see where it would help him much.

The committee was split about what *The Review* should report. They wanted the publicity, but I was having a hard time convincing them that lists of statistics would likely have as avid a readership as the daily farm report would in Manhattan.

One man explained, "You don't understand, Ms. Walker. We can't just let you write about our clients. The information is confidential."

"I do understand, but if the story isn't about people, then people won't want to read it."

We had reached an impasse when Judy, a delegate from the Denver police, intervened.

"We are going to be conducting a police intervention at several area brothels within the next week. I can't tell you where or when. But if you are willing to be on standby, we could call you in soon enough that you could interview the women, take pictures and view the brothel. You would need to keep the identities of the women confidential. And you wouldn't be able to talk with them until they were done with their police interviews. But it might give you and your readers a good picture of these places and what the lives of these women are like."

Latif was half way out of his chair in protest as I shouted, "That would be great."

"How is that great?" he said. "These women are traumatized and afraid. How is it great to have a reporter prodding at them at a time like that?"

"Give me some credit, Latif. It's not like I'm going to bring a whip and thumb screws. I couldn't be a reporter if I couldn't be tactful when needed."

"I hadn't noticed."

"Latif," Judy interjected, "be reasonable. If we want the publicity, we are going to have to give access. You know Jo is right. You'll get a lot more interest, and maybe even funding, if people can understand this problem on a personal level."

Latif sat back down, but didn't say anything. I had the distinct feeling I'd just won the battle but might have lost the war. I was likely going to get an interesting story. But it sure didn't look like I'd won any of Latif's lasting gratitude.

The meeting ended with Judy and Latif huddled in a corner in heated debate. My only attempt to join the conversation was rebuffed by a hostile look from Latif and a faint head shake from Judy. I decided to leave the convincing to her. I tucked my mobile phone number in her hand. Then I ducked out the nearest door to avoid another glad hand from Mark Miller.

The call from Judy came two days later. It was early evening. The sun barely set. I jumped in my car and drove to a commercial district not far from downtown Denver. The police were already loading several young women into a van with Latif riding escort. There didn't seem to be any other civilians around.

Judy walked up to me.

"Latif is not going to let you talk to those women until he's had some time with them and gotten their permission."

"But the idea was for me to interview them here where they worked. I mean, how many of them are going to be willing to talk with me afterward?"

"Not many. Maybe none. I know. But this is Latif's operation and he's not one to trust people he doesn't know well."

"What a jerk. I'm surprised he gets to know anybody well."

I could see from Judy's expression that she didn't appreciate my criticism of Latif.

"Listen, I'm sorry. It just seems like you guys want my help, but you want me to give it with one hand tied behind my back. I know Latif does important work. But he frustrates me."

"He's so protective that he's an obstacle," Judy nodded. "But try to look at it this way, Jo. Latif may be the only man who's tried to protect these women in years, maybe their whole lives. If you want his help, you're going to need to meet him where his priorities are, not yours. Let me take you through the brothel. You may find enough heartache there to interest your readers."

That last was said with a hardness that shook me. I decided not to respond. No one wanted to hear my defenses. My actions would need to win over more than Latif apparently. I was determined that they would.

Judy led me into the building that housed the brothel.

I don't know what I had expected, a lavish room lit with soft light, draped with red velvet. A long spiral staircase. A cross between a sultan's harem and a western saloon with young women draped in elegant gowns or silk kimonos hanging over aged oak banisters. Well, not that. But I wasn't expecting this.

This could have been a waiting room in any office.

Metal chairs lined the walls. End tables were stacked with magazines, overflowing ashtrays and half-empty drink glasses. I could imagine the men sitting back reading, legs crossed, flipping the ash from cigarettes, stopping to check their watches, leaning forward to share a joke, a story while they waited. Waited for what? Their turn with a sixteen-year-old girl hidden in a back room?

I turned to Judy. "Where?" I choked out.

She opened a door and pointed up a flight of stairs.

The bedrooms were worse. They were divided into small cubicles, marked off only with hanging curtains. Each woman had her place. One metal cot. No sheets. No blankets. Clothes piled on chairs or folded in piles on the floor.

I looked for signs of life. Where was the small, many-folded, carefully guarded and cherished family picture? Where were the cheap trinkets, the dime store jewelry carelessly tossed at these women, but treasured as promises of a future life or remembrances of a tender moment? I felt desperate to find something. Something to say that a woman had lived here, that a child had lived here. I came expecting to find young women trapped in a life of despair but holding on to a hope for something better. But I was wrong. This was not a life lived in desperation. This was a life lived without hope. There were no ties to a former life. There were no icons for the future. There was only the present. The unrelenting present with all its pain and tedium.

How had Angela ever found her way out of this living death? Was death a worse fate? For me it seemed that it was, but only because I couldn't imagine living without hope. But if you truly had no hope that a life like this would ever change? I just couldn't answer that question. It was so far beyond my experience.

But I knew that somewhere Angela had found the strength to resist. Where had she hidden her hope? How had she kept it alive?

She was the one who had found something to hold up against the despair. The strong ones are not the survivors. Who had said that? Frankel — seeing the good even in the most awful places. It is not always the best who survive. I know that. I know that is how they work. Kill the resisters. Make an example. But I couldn't accept it. They had killed the one woman, the one child who dared to hope. And I would see them destroyed for it.

But being here looking at the remnants of these empty lives raised another question.

"Judy, why would anyone kill Angela? What could she possibly have had that anyone could have wanted? Would they have killed her just to make an example?"

"Possibly, but not likely. She was young and attractive from what we can tell. By killing her, they were throwing away a lot of money. Maybe it was an accident. Maybe they were trying to take her back and the violence got out of hand."

"Is that what you think happened?"

"I don't know, Jo. Could have been an out-of-control customer or it could have been a pissed off pimp. These young women live in a violent world. We may never know exactly why she died."

I knew Judy was right. But it wasn't a good enough answer. Maybe I never would know why. But someone knew. And I wasn't going to stop looking until I'd run every possible lead to ground. So much for my pledge to Hazel to let the police handle it. Hazel knew me better than I knew myself.

For now I was going to go find Latif and get those interviews I needed so I could write a story that would melt even his cold reserve.

Chapter Twelve

Despite my best efforts, I wasn't able to track down Latif. He and the women from the raid disappeared into the bowels of the Denver Police Department. I thought of calling Russ, but decided I'd pretty much burned that bridge until I had something to offer in trade.

As a last resort, I planted myself on the floor outside Latif's office with a thick novel and a pint of ice cream. The ice cream was gone and the plot just thickening when Latif walked up. He stared down at me with a look I wouldn't describe as welcoming.

"Well, I can't say I'm surprised. I can't say I'm pleased either. Come on in."

We entered his office where he perched on a corner of his desk, scattering papers to the floor.

"You can't talk to the women from the raid today."

"We had a deal, Latif. You provide the sources. I provide the story."

"Well, your sources are in jail and they've lawyered up."

"How could they afford lawyers?"

"Does that surprise you?"

"Well, no, I guess not." Likely there was someone footing the bill to get them back to work. "Is there any way I can get in to see them?"

"No."

"Well, is there a way to find out who paid for the lawyers?"

"You're supposed to be writing a story about the brothels, remember? Not investigating the people behind them. What do I have to say to get you to back off? Besides, I don't know of a way to find the guy paying for the defense. Lawyers generally don't share their client lists. I suppose you could go to the law firm and harass the receptionist till she breaks down. You seem to have a gift for harassment."

It was only the faintest smile, but I saw it fleet across his eyes. A crack in the ice.

"How about a second-hand source for your story? The woman I told you about, the one who knew the murdered girl, Angela. Her name is Rosa. I could ask her if she'd be willing to talk with you. Complete confidentiality though. No pictures, no names. And I mean for you to talk with her just about this story you're writing. I don't want you dragging her into any mess you make digging around in the murder investigation."

I knew it was an enormous concession. I felt like I'd just opened a locked door.

"That would be great, Latif."

He looked at me like he was trying to use my eyes as windows into my brain.

"Don't be going and getting all enthusiastic. I don't trust you, Walker. I've never met a reporter who could place the people before the story. But Hazel says you can. If you play Rosa false, Hazel will have a lot to answer for. I'll call you later tonight to set up a time, if Rosa agrees. We'll need to meet someplace private, maybe Hazel's house. I'll let you know."

It wasn't Latif who called later that night. It was Hazel.

"Latif set up the meeting with Rosa for tomorrow morning here at my place, 10:00 a.m. Jo, Latif isn't convinced that you see the danger in what is going on here. He asked me to talk with you again to be sure you understand that you are dealing with dangerous people. It's not just you he's worried about. He doesn't want Rosa pulled back into the crosshairs of these people. She disappeared as far as they're concerned, and he wants it to stay that way."

"Hazel, of course I know it's dangerous. A woman is dead. I went to the brothel. I saw what these guys are willing to do to make a buck. I know they are dangerous. That's why they have to be stopped."

"Jo, that just sounds like empty words to me. Do you know it in your gut?"

"I do. And I have no intention of exposing Rosa. You know I wouldn't do that."

"Well, remember Rosa does know to be afraid. She knows it down to every cell in her body. Respect that fear, and learn from it. If you go into this conversation with anything less, she won't trust you. And if she doesn't trust you, she won't tell you anything. She can't afford to. Goodnight, Jo. Sleep well. I'll see you in the morning."

After a conversation like that, I had a hard time getting any sleep at all. The night passed slowly. Of course I wanted Rosa to trust me. But I also wanted information about Angela, and Latif had put that conversation out of bounds. So I was going to have to dig around for illicit information, with Latif watching over my shoulder, while I appeared honest and trustworthy so Rosa would confide in me and Latif wouldn't bodily throw me out of the house. Could tomorrow be any more fun?

Next morning Hazel met me at the door with a cup of coffee. I'd already had three and was working up some serious stomach acid. But I took it. Something warm to hold on to seemed like just the thing at the moment.

"Latif and Rosa are both here. They're in the living room. I'm going to take myself out to the deck in back."

"You're not coming in?"

"No, I think Rosa will do better without the extra audience."

Sure, maybe Rosa would, but I had hoped for some moral support in facing Latif. It looked like I was on my own.

When Latif and I had spoken about Rosa, I pictured an older, more mature woman, someone who'd had the time and experience to discover a way to leave the brothels. When I saw her sitting ramrod straight on Hazel's couch, I knew my mistake. Rosa wasn't more than a year or two older than Angela had been, maybe 18. She had a medium-height, stocky build. Not particularly attractive, but with thick, black hair and large, deep brown eyes. I could have sat down and cried just looking at her. Children . . . these were just children. But Rosa wasn't inviting pity or even sympathy. There was something wise about her, or maybe it was a worldliness. My pity would earn her scorn, not her respect.

I turned to Latif, who was wearing the look of a mama grizzly bear.

"Rosa," he said, "this is Jo Walker from *The Review*. Walker, this is Rosa Esposito. She's agreed to talk with you about what it was like living in a brothel. She gets complete anonymity and that's the extent of this interview. Any problem with those conditions?"

My patience was running a little thin with Latif and his rules.

"Look, we discussed this already yesterday and yes, I agree." I looked at Rosa. "If that's what you'd like, Ms. Esposito, that's what we'll do."

"Please, call me Rosa." She looked at Latif. "Latif, would you mind leaving us? I'd rather speak with Ms. Walker alone."

Latif looked like he'd been swatted on his ursine nose. He hadn't expected this. Still, he got up and left the room. A moment later the back door snapped shut. Sounded like Hazel had company on the deck.

"He thinks he has to protect me from you, Ms. Walker, though you don't look all that dangerous."

"Please call me Jo. He's afraid that I'll write something that will make you a threat to the people who run the brothels where you used to work. Or, that I'll drag you into my investigation of Angela's death."

"That's why I wanted to talk with you alone. Do you think you can find out who killed her? Can you bring the murderer to justice?"

Justice. It was such a naive question. Straight out of a TV cop show.

"I don't know if I can figure out who killed her. I'm going to do my best. But even if I do, I can't promise justice. That's out of my hands."

"But you'll try?"

"I'll do what I can, Rosa, but that may not be much. Why do you ask?"

"Angela was a friend. Many of the girls in the brothel were like friends. As much as we could be. And no one tries to get justice for them. Latif tries to save them, the police try to shut down the brothels. But that's not justice for the harm that's been done. Me, the other girls, we're too afraid to seek justice. Even when we get out, we just want to hide, to get away. But Angela's dead. They can't hurt her anymore. At least for this one of us there could be justice. I will tell you what I know about Angela and about the men who run the brothels if you will tell me that you will try for this justice."

I was stunned by her outburst. I suppose, like the others, I'd thought that closing the brothels, getting the women to safety was enough. But of course it wasn't. The past couldn't be erased, but it could be exposed, acknowledged. Payment needed to be made.

"One more thing I will tell you about Angela," Rosa began again, "in case maybe it could help you with your investigation to know this. She had a cell phone, one that she stole from a man who had been with her. She had taken pictures on this phone, pictures that showed what kind of man this really was . . . what a bad, bad man he is. She wanted to trade this phone back to him for her freedom. She asked for my help, but I told her there was nothing I would know how to do. I told her to take it to Latif, and I gave her his phone number and address of his office. If anyone could help her, it would be Latif. But when I asked him if she ever came to him, he said no, he never heard from her. Maybe that's what she was trying to do when they killed her."

"Did you see the pictures, Rosa?" I asked.

She shook her head.

"I did not want to see pictures like that. I wouldn't have known who the man is anyway. But if Latif had seen them, he might have known how to find out. If there was some way you could find this phone, if they haven't already destroyed it, maybe it could help."

I tried to digest this information, but under the circumstances couldn't think what I might do with it.

Rosa and I talked for two hours. I could just picture Latif pacing a hole through Hazel's deck. I got more than enough background for my story. Rosa confirmed she was smuggled into the country by Carlos Rivera. Her description of the man who brought her to the brothel fit the man who had vandalized my car to a tee, right down to the pocked face and sneering smile. His name was Luis and it was him who first raped her. Who first made her understand what her new life was going to be like. So that ties Rivera to the brothels, at least indirectly, I thought.

I recalled his smug, contrived outrage at our interview, and I felt I was ready to nail the guy.

The conversation exhausted me. My initial anger faded into weariness as Rosa recounted the daily abuse and hopelessness.

Finally we wound to an end when I couldn't find the heart to ask more questions. I had heard all I could bear.

Latif and Rosa left. I said a hasty goodbye to Hazel, not wanting the comfort I knew she would offer. I needed to be alone.

Chapter Thirteen

I spent the next four hours alone in my office, pounding all my frustration and anger into my computer. If I'd had any Scotch, I would have been downing it with gusto. But I didn't, and at the moment that seemed like a real disadvantage. I was out of ideas. I'd pretty much promised Rosa that I would charge off in pursuit of that elusive ideal called justice, like Galahad in search of the Holy Grail. I just didn't know where to find it.

Well, if I couldn't ride off with lance and shield I could use the mighty pen. I was composing paragraphs that dripped of venom and accusation enough to make a rapper blanch. Unpublishable of course, but getting it out on paper was clearing my head. Clearing my head, but not moving me any closer to my goal. What next?

Latif didn't really want to help me. He just wanted a news story that would get him his funding and then have me fade into oblivion. Russ wasn't talking to me since I'd dodged him at the rally. Hazel wanted to protect, not assist me. I was short on allies. As for adversaries, I had plenty of those. But none seemed to fit the bill for murder. I'd decided that Duffet was noxious but not involved, except of course as a perpetrator of hate. There was Rivera and his cohorts. I could have gotten frostbite from the cold shoulder he had given me. I didn't expect he'd be much interested in helping me. Well, in all fairness, why would he be if he was breaking the law smuggling prostitutes into the country?

Of course I didn't necessarily need his cooperation so much as evidence of what he was up to. I packed up my computer, grabbed my coat, a bag of Cheetos and a bottle of water from the vending machine, and headed to my car. I'd already been to Rivera's office. Maybe it was time to look closer to home. There had to be a physical connection between him and the brothels.

How was the transportation arranged? How was the money collected and transferred? Of course, even if I could prove his connection to the brothels, that didn't connect him to the murder. Well, that could come later. If I could nail him for the prostitution at least it would feel like payback for the damage to my car.

A quick web search had told me where to find Rivera's house in the Belcaro neighborhood of Denver. It was adjacent to the green belt that ran along Cherry Creek, and within walking distance to the Cherry Creek Mall. I grabbed a space in the mall parking lot and hoofed it to the creek. In minutes I was huddled beside a tree, staring into Rivera's living room. People who live in glass houses shouldn't throw stones. They also shouldn't run clandestine operations. The back of the house was a sheet of glass with panoramic views to the private swimming pool, Cherry Creek, and the mountains beyond.

Beautiful but not great planning. If I had brought a pair of binoculars I'd be able to see what the family was eating for dinner. Reminder to self . . . next time bring binoculars. In the meantime I was more interested in seeing who had come for dinner. My Rottweiler friend from the interview was standing on an upper balcony, staring out to the river. That was a little spooky. At the dinner table Rivera, his wife and three kids were sharing a meal with my friend Luis, the guy who broke into my car near the skate park. Did these two thugs live with Rivera? Not the company I'd choose for my kids.

It didn't look like much else was going to happen here tonight and I was catching a chill. Even in spring, nights are not warm in Denver. When the sun goes down the temperature drops. I'd have to prepare better and come back tomorrow night. Better snacks and warmer clothes . . . oh yeah, and binoculars.

I woke at noon the next day to, of all things, the sounds of the Beach Boys. Today was Bill's picnic. With all that had been going on, I'd simply forgotten my promise to attend. I was still feeling tired and drained. But the muted voices and music from next door seemed to offer some refuge from my weary frustration. Escape was a good option. I headed for the shower.

Bill must have meant it when he said he was inviting everyone he knew. His yard was crowded with children and adults. Most were standing by tables that were covered with food and drink. Others were battling in the badminton court or swimming in the pool — brave souls for a spring day. Among the happily jostling people I could just make out Hazel. She was regaling Bill with some story that had them both bursting with laughter. I felt some of the tension draining from me. God, it was good seeing people laugh. It made the world seem a bit less grim than I had been imagining it lately.

Bill left Hazel and headed in my direction.

"Hey Jo, I'm glad you could make it."

"So am I, Bill. Looks like everyone is having a blast. Is Linda here yet?"

The change in Bill's expression was subtle, moving into a small frown.

"No, Jessie came over with Hazel, but no Linda."

I smiled at him.

"Give it time. She's probably somewhere making lists of the pros and cons. She'll show up."

Bill looked startled but didn't pursue the topic.

"There's someone I'd like you to meet over this way," he said, pointing.

He led me to the grill where a large man was flipping hamburgers, watched intently by none other than Bosco the dog.

"Hey Ben, I'd like you to meet Jo, my next door neighbor, the newspaper reporter I've mentioned. Jo, this is Ben, the best vet in Denver. We just call him Bear. Thought you guys might like to get acquainted," he said with a mischievous smile at Ben. Clearly I had been a topic of conversation before this. "Well, I've got to run and check on things, but Ben can fix you up with something to eat." With that, Bill rushed off.

Ben's smile was as big as he was.

"Well, that was subtle, wasn't it?"

I smiled back.

"Not very, but I'm sure his heart is in the right place."

"A little less heart and a lot more tact would be nice. So, can I interest you in a burger?" he said pointing at the grill.

"Sure. Should I really call you Bear?"

"Please don't," he said with a laugh. "Bill is the only one who has ever called me Bear. He just keeps hoping it'll stick."

I laughed too. There was something appealing about Ben. He felt expansive, like an open meadow on a summer day in the mountains. I could imagine animals feeling safe with him . . . no pushing, just all the space you need to feel safe and heal. I was surprised to find myself vaguely jealous of his patients.

God knows I could use a wide open space to feel safe. Healing? That seemed far off.

"How long have you known Bill?"

"Since we were kids. We lived in the same neighborhood. He was the older kid that I kind of idolized and kept chasing after. Funny when I think back on it. He was good about it though. He let me tag along with him and his friends even though I was really too young for them. Then when I was working my way through college,

I worked summers in his Dad's plumbing company. I was there when Bill came back. That was when our friendship really took hold."

"Came back?" I asked. "From where?"

"Afghanistan. He hasn't told you?"

I shook my head, and Ben nodded.

"I should have realized that. No offense, but it's not something he talks about much until he knows you really well."

"No offense taken," I said.

"There were some rough times for Bill back then. But that's long gone now," he said, shaking his head. I could see him cast around for a new topic.

"I see you've met Bosco," I said, pointing to the dog.

"Oh yeah, he's been by the grill supervising since I started cooking. That is one smart dog."

"Linda already has his college tuition saved up, though she's hoping for a scholarship."

Ben smiled, and then looking a bit sheepish asked, "So, what do you think of Linda and Bill, as a couple I mean? She seems flighty."

Of all the words in the English language, flighty is not one I would ever have thought to apply to Linda.

Ben noticed my surprise and added, "Maybe flighty isn't exactly the word. But she's like a light bulb. One minute she's on, the next minute she's off. Just look at her talking with Bill. She's smiling like a school girl, but if she were standing back any further she'd need a megaphone for him to hear her."

I looked over to where he was pointing. Linda had arrived. Ben's description was right on. She laughed with Bill, resting a hand on his arm, while the whole rest of her body was turned in the opposite direction looking like it was about to sprint off for home.

I paused for a moment, not quite sure how to explain Linda's behavior to Ben.

"Linda had one of the happiest marriages I've ever seen. Her husband, Larry, was an artist. They met when she was in law school in New York. He was working at a gallery in the village. It was one of those small co-op studios where the artists run the place. Linda didn't have much of a background in art. Her father was more of a Remington man. Good, easy-to-understand Western art. Larry's paintings were massive swirls of color. I think they literally swept her off her feet. She would go down to the gallery every time she got a break from class. Then she'd come back and call me in Boston where I was in grad school to tell me how outrageous the paintings were, how they didn't make any sense. She'd storm around her dorm room till she was worn out. Then she'd just sit and say something like, 'But you know it would sure look nice on that wall.' I don't think anyone was more surprised when they got married than Linda. But they were great for each other."

"What happened?"

"He was killed in a car accident three years ago. Linda hasn't had a romantic relationship since then. And I don't think she expects to have another one."

Ben frowned.

"It doesn't look like my man Bill has much chance then, huh?"

"I don't know. They're a lot alike."

It was Ben's turn to be surprised.

"Bill and Linda are a lot alike?"

"No, Bill and Larry."

"How so?"

"Well let me put it this way. Linda's life gets to be like a motel room . . . efficient, orderly, clean, but basically dreary. She needs someone to come in every once in a while and make a mess. Larry always kept Linda from falling into ruts. And from what I know of Bill, I'm sure he's good for adding a bit of mayhem to a cozy life."

Ben smiled, "Well I guess that explains your friendship."

"Yeah," I said ruefully, "I tend to make messes, too."

"How about you," Ben asked. "Ever thought of giving marriage a try?"

"Sure, I did it once. Lasted about 2 years. We just kind of drifted apart."

"That's pretty fast drifting." He smiled.

"Yeah, well, I guess there wasn't much holding us together in the first place. How about you?"

"No, not yet. I always planned to get married, but it just hasn't happened. I'm still hopeful though."

"Well, good luck with that. Somehow I can't imagine fitting a relationship into my life."

"Bill tells me you're working on a big immigration story."

"Maybe. Right now I can't tell if it's immigration, prostitution, or something completely off my radar. Looks like all three rolled into one big mess. And, honestly, I'm having a heck of a time figuring it all out."

"You'll get there. But not today. This is official downtime. What say we leave the grill to Bosco and anyone who wants to cook their own burger and go annoy Bill and Linda? Who knows, maybe we can nudge them into a real date."

Before we reached that goal, Hazel intercepted us. She was accompanied by Cap, her sort of man friend, though I don't think I quite understand the relationship. Cap is an ex–Captain in the Denver police force, hence the moniker. He didn't seem like the kind of guy Hazel would hang out with. But predicting Hazel is akin to predicting Denver weather. You just never know what to expect. She took my arm and waved Ben aside. He immediately trotted off smiling. Wow, I needed to master that skill. Maybe I could wave Duffet away with a flick of my hand.

"I wanted to check in with you. The way you bolted from my

house yesterday, I figured the interview with Rosa must have been rough."

"Well sure, stories of rape and abuse always lift my spirits."

"Don't be snide. It doesn't fit you. Did you learn anything helpful?"

"Yes. Rosa verified that it was Rivera who smuggled her and Angela into the country. And I saw the guy she described as taking her to the brothel at Rivera's house last night. And honestly, how does a civil servant like Rivera afford a multi-million dollar house in Belcaro anyhow? The man reeks of corruption."

"Can you take what you have to the police?"

Here she looked at Cap. So that explained why he was in this conversation. Nudging me to hand my investigation over. But he didn't jump in.

"Of course not. I can't prove anything. And they are not going to want to mess with someone with Rivera's clout. I'm going to keep camping out in his backyard until something concrete turns up."

"Tell me you don't mean his literal backyard."

"Don't ask and I won't tell." With a smile I added, "I could use a stack of sandwiches for tonight."

"I am not provisioning any such expedition. You can get your sandwiches at 7-11 and risk ptomaine before I'd be an accomplice."

Chapter Fourteen

Day Two of the stakeout and my spirits were dropping with the temperature. Not that I was cold. I could have trudged through the Alaska winter in my current getup. I had more to fear from heat stroke than hypothermia. But I was bored. And hungry since Hazel had not come through with the sandwiches. Staking out a house in the dark was a whole lot less interesting than I'd imagined, and it had already been way down on my list of interesting things to do. If someone didn't come out of Rivera's house soon I was going to call it quits.

Patience isn't my strong suit. The only thing that kept me sitting there was that I couldn't come up with another plan. I was cranky and sleep-deprived. And nothing was happening. The house was dark except for the security lights around the perimeter. No one stirred, not even a mouse.

I had settled on the ground and was nodding in my parka well past midnight when movement through the hedge caught my attention. It looked like Luis, the shorter of the two thugs that I had learned often flanked Rivera. Well, well, Luis, where would you be going in the wee hours of the morning with that manila envelope nestled under your arm?

Probably out for a pack of cigarettes, the way my nights were going. Still, I'd be asleep in the mulch if I didn't move soon. Luis climbed behind the wheel of a black SUV. Day-Glo orange would have suited me better, but felons tend to avoid the color. Time to put my plan into action -- follow the bad guy to some all-revealing destination and crack the case. Way too many episodes of NCIS in my entertainment history.

I'd never tailed a car before. It's just not the kind of thing that comes up a lot in life: the need to furtively follow felons around dark streets. But I'd watched enough cop shows that I figured I had the general idea. Feeling like a poor imitation of a paperback detective, I sprinted through the hedge and around the corner to where I'd parked my car on the street. No mall parking lot this time. I wanted to be in sprinting distance. I crawled nearly prone into the front seat. First rule of tailing, don't let the guy see you climbing into your car in haste as he pulls from the driveway. Luckily, Luis seemed intent on his errand.

Following him through the deserted neighborhood streets was not easy. I knew that another pair of headlights would arouse suspicion. On the other hand, a car driving around with lights off in the dark would be a lot worse. So I wove in and out through the neighborhood, driving parallel streets and occasionally cutting back across his path, checking that he hadn't turned off. It was nerve wracking. I covered three times the distance he did and lost him twice. But both times I found him by frantically driving in circles until I caught sight of the SUV. It got easier when he pulled onto the interstate and headed west out of town. Well, clearly this wasn't a cigarette trip. I just hoped it wasn't a spring skiing weekend in Aspen. Of course I hadn't seen any skis, so that probably wasn't his destination.

It was another 20 minutes before he exited the highway and headed through a maze of office buildings and small commercial storefronts south of the interstate. In a short time he was pulling into the long driveway leading into an office complex. This was not going to work. There was no way I could drive up to the buildings without him seeing me. I cut the lights and drove slowly to a dark corner of the complex and parked my car in the first space I could find. Luis had already driven around the corner of one of the buildings. I could only hope he wouldn't notice that a car hadn't been there when he pulled in. I trusted the dark to conceal both me and the car. I slid from the front seat, grabbed my camera from the back seat and headed out across the parking lot.

Feeling more and more like a paperback detective, I dodged through trees and snuck around corners. I didn't find Luis, but his car was parked in front of one of the buildings. I crawled to the side and peeked in. No manila envelope, no skis either. I couldn't imagine a brothel in this building. If there was one, business was bad. The SUV was one of only two cars in the parking lot. The other was a silver Mercedes sedan. Still no Day-Glo. I jotted down its license plate number on an off chance, headed into the shrubbery and settled back into the hedge.

Most office complexes are basically the same: lots of parking, fiercely tailored landscaping, tall buildings. But oddly, this office complex was looking familiar . . . I just couldn't place it.

Then it hit me: why I knew this building. I just hadn't recognized it in the dark. This was the office building where Dorothea Messenger had her in-state congressional office. I'd been here a half dozen times knocking on her door trying for an interview. It had to be a coincidence. There was no way the guardian of moral rectitude would have any dealings with a human trafficker, or even with a liberal politician for that matter. The idea was ludicrous. But it was a mighty curious coincidence.

I was still arguing with myself about Messenger in the role of brothel madam when the door opened and Jacob Shaw walked out, followed closely by Luis, the pair engaged in apparently tense conversation. Messenger's top aide meeting with Rivera's muscle man? My brain skidded to a complete halt. If I had tried to talk, dithering would have poured out. There was no way. It was like being handed the pieces of two different jigsaw puzzles and trying to make them into a single picture. But I did have the presence of mind to quickly raise my digital camera, zoom in near enough to be able to identify faces, and snap three or four pictures in rapid succession just before they both slammed into their cars and roared off.

There was no way I could make it back to my car in time to follow one of them. And besides, which one?

They were both long gone by the time I collected myself enough to stand up. I headed for my car and cell phone. Hazel might be avoiding me, but I needed to talk with her right now. She was the only person I could think of who could help me make sense of this. There was something seriously wrong here, some mischief afoot, and Hazel would believe that.

Chapter Fifteen

The next morning I was at Messenger's office early. I'd spoken with Hazel last night. She was as confused as I was. Neither one of us could come up with any reason for one of Rivera's men to meet in the middle of the night with Messenger's aide. Hazel promised to send feelers out to her network. But I wasn't feeling patient. I'd been stymied in this investigation for so long I was in the mood to kick the ant hill to see what crawled out.

With the grand lady in town, Messenger's office was abuzz with activity. The reception desk fronted an area filled with cubicles, where people rushed back and forth consumed with their own business. I stood in front of the desk for five minutes waiting to be noticed. Finally I got an exasperated look from a young girl attached to a telephone.

"How can I help you?" she said.

I handed her my press card and asked to see Shaw. As she placed the call to his extension, I realized I hadn't thought this through very carefully. What was I going to do? Ask the man if Messenger had a secret alliance with Rivera? I could just imagine it, Rivera bringing in more and more illegal immigrants so that Messenger could have more and more ammunition for her tirades. No, I was going to need some kind of smoke screen to get any information. While I was planning my lies, the receptionist got off the phone.

"I'm sorry, Mr. Shaw isn't in the office."

"Oh, come on, I saw his car in the parking lot," I blurted out. It probably wasn't my smartest move, to let it be known that I knew his car. After all, the only reason I had recognized it when I drove in was because I'd seen him drive off in it last night. But the statement fell out before I could stop it. I was that frustrated.

Clearly this young girl was not accustomed to lying. Guilt flushed across her face. But, she was loyal.

"Well, I can't speak to that," she said. "Maybe you'd like to call later and make an appointment with his secretary."

"How about if you send me back now and I'll make that appointment?"

"I'm sorry, but his secretary isn't available either," she said.

It wasn't hard to recognize that I was getting the cold shoulder. But, I was feeling obstinate.

"Well then, I'll just wait till she is."

"No, you can't wait," she stammered.

I had to admire her stalwartness. She clearly was in serious violation of her parentally ingrained standard of politeness. But she wasn't about to disobey her orders. Someone must have been pretty darn adamant about not letting me past the front desk. I was going to need to move on to Plan B, which was gaining appeal by the minute. I turned to leave the office but couldn't resist one parting shot.

"I can't imagine why you would work for someone who would make you lie for them. It doesn't seem very moral."

The girl's face crumbled, and I left feeling like a heel. Well, sometimes I just am a heel. I could live with that. All the better for my next step, I thought.

I made a quick survey of the office as I left, noting the location of the copy room. Shaw and his secretary must be hidden behind one of the two oak doors behind the cubicle area. Both the doors had locks; so did the front door into the office. Damn. On the other hand I didn't see any sign of an alarm. I was planning a late night visit to this office. It was not going to be easy, but it was possible. Good, I was definitely in the mood to do some bad to Shaw.

I spent the rest of my day trying to talk myself out of a break-in to Shaw's office. I don't think of myself as a criminal. I believe in law. It's just that when the law conflicts with digging out the truth, the truth wins hands down with me. That's not a standard I would necessarily recommend for society. It's just the way I'm wired. I had to admit, though, there was more going on here than high ideals of truth and justice. I was just plain annoyed. I didn't like Shaw with his moral self-righteousness, never had. The idea of catching him in the wrong added a little spring to my step. Seemed like a good enough reason for a break-in to me.

It was just starting to get dark when I headed out to Messenger's office. I'd brought along a thermos of coffee and stopped at the market on the way for a sandwich, a bag of chips, and a box of Oreos. It's always good to have snacks along when committing a felony. It helps ease the tension. Besides, I was expecting a long wait.

Getting into the office building was easy. I left my car in a dark corner of the parking lot after throwing some mud on the license plate, a trick I picked up from Magnum PI or some such detective show. I walked into the building just before it closed and headed for the ladies room.

This would be the hard part, the waiting. I sat in a booth, pulled out a paperback and the chips and settled in for the evening. I could only hope this wasn't the day the cleaning crew mopped up the bathroom.

In that regard my luck held. No one came into the restroom, and after waiting till midnight I decided it was safe to see if the building was deserted.

I took the elevator to the top floor and then went floor by floor checking for lights beneath the office doors. I didn't want to be disturbed by any late night wanderers. For my last stop I returned to the third floor, where Messenger's office was. The only illumination was the dull emergency lights placed sparingly in the hallway.

I'd picked up my burglary skills back in Boston from one of my news sources. He was an old guy who spent more of his time in prison than out of it. He saw himself as a kind of roguish Robin Hood. I saw him as a lonely old scam artist. He thought if I had a better skill set I would understand him better, that I might even write a feature article about him that could lead to a book deal that would set him up for life. He was just one of those optimists who can't help but hope for the best in any situation. He spent hours teaching me how to pick locks, pockets, and marks for a scam. The lessons stopped when one of his jobs landed him back in prison. I did write an article about him, but I didn't hear whether he ever got that book deal.

I'd never needed to pick pockets or marks, but this wasn't the first time I'd been alone with a set of lock picks in a dark hallway. I sat down in front of the door to Messenger's office, pulled out my flashlight and lock picks, and slipped on a pair of latex gloves. Looked like your basic pin–and–tumbler design. I stuck the torsion wrench and hook pick in the keyhole and set to work. I timed myself at twenty-two minutes. I never said I was good at breaking and entering, just mildly experienced.

There was not a sound or a soul in Messenger's domain. I turned on the flashlight and walked through the outer office towards the doors to the inner sanctum, stopping only long enough to flip on the copy machine just in case something interesting needed copying.

Back to the lock picks. I picked the right–hand door. Just

seemed like poetry that Shaw should be on the right side of the office. This time I made it through in sixteen minutes. Whatever happened, the night would not be a total loss . . . my lock picking skills were improving. And my instinct was right. In front of me was a secretary's desk. The doorway to Shaw's office was clearly marked behind it. Luckily his office door was open. I might actually finish here before daybreak.

I started at Shaw's desk, pulling out drawers, leafing through papers. Not much there. The only thing of interest was a list of donations with letters from contributors, all singing praise or asking favors. Duffet was on the list for a measly $1,000. There was no mention of Rivera. It seemed strange to me that donor information would be left sitting in an unlocked drawer. But given the disclosure requirements of federal campaign finance laws, I could probably get the same information on the web. Still, I put the list aside to make a copy.

There was a docking station for a laptop, but no computer. Shaw must have taken it home. Figures. He wasn't the kind of guy who could let the world continue even for an evening without his surveillance. It was just as well. I'm not someone who can hack a password, and this way I didn't have to waste time trying. If the information I needed was on the computer, so be it. I resumed my search with waning enthusiasm.

All that remained was the file cabinet. It could take a day to go through every file and I just didn't have the time. I considered just giving it a pass. Instead I decided to scan the folders to see if any labels jumped out. I reached to pull out the top drawer. It was locked. The other three pulled out easily. Well, where would Shaw be likely to hide any secrets? Most likely in a locked drawer. My enthusiasm returned with a blast. Back to the lock picks.

The drawer held only forty or so hanging files. I did a quick scan eliminating half as irrelevant. I swept up the rest and headed to the copy machine. Half an hour later I had everything back in place and was on my way to the front door. I didn't have any way to lock the doors behind me. I could only hope that no one noticed or it was blown off as carelessness. I hoped the young receptionist didn't catch the blame, but then being fired from this place wasn't the worst thing that could happen. Maybe she could find a job that would expand her mind rather than slamming it shut.

With that cheerful thought I headed out of the office just in time to hear the elevator doors opening. I dove back inside looking for a place to hide. I could barely hear footsteps in the carpeted hallway. Someone was walking from office to office jiggling each doorknob as they passed. It must be a security service. Of course a building like this would have a nightly walk-through.

I briefly wondered if the guard was armed. Of course I had other questions too. Had he noticed my car in the parking lot? Had he wiped off the mud and written down my license plate number? Was this his first time through tonight, or had he already checked earlier and knew the doors were locked at that time?

I curled up in a cubicle under a desk, pulling the chair behind me to block a clear view. Not the best hiding place. But, I assured myself, this was not the Secret Service I was dealing with. This was some guy making minimum wage for a job that could get him killed. How motivated could he be?

The office lights flashed on as he walked in. "Anybody in here?"

Well, that was a good sign. He was expecting a late night worker, not a break in.

I heard him rummaging through the cubicles. I was imagining myself as a tiny speck of dust while trying not to breathe loudly. He walked to the back and I heard him open the door to Shaw's office. This was my chance. I squirmed out of my hiding place and stuck my head around the corner. I could hear him moving in the back offices, but I couldn't see him. I figured that worked both ways. I crept to the door, keeping my eyes focused for movement in the back. Just as I reached the door the guard walked into the front office. I ran through the door and bolted down the hallway. I wasn't sure if he had seen me. I didn't think so. But I wasn't chancing the noise of the elevator. I made for the stairwell and flew down three flights of stairs faster than a fox in a hunt, which was just how I was feeling.

I sprinted for the car. Turning, I could see that the lights were still on in Messenger's office. So either he'd run out right behind me or he was continuing his search, probably calling for backup.

I started my car, and leaving the headlights off pulled slowly from my parking spot. There was no sign of pursuit. I knew it was standard security policy to check cars left in a lot overnight. I could only hope my friend had skipped that part or had been waiting until after the office check. If he had taken my license number and he reported a burglary, or even just that the doors were left unlocked, I might well be visiting with the police for a bit of questioning. Good thing my BGF was a lawyer.

But if they had been called, the police didn't show up at the office complex in time to find me there. I was back on the highway heading home and there was no sign of pursuit. Time to think up a darn good reason for my car to have been abandoned in the parking lot. I pulled out my cell phone and placed a call to Hazel. It would have been kinder to wait until morning. But she's a master at misdirecting the police. I needed a few pointers, and the sooner the better. Then I had a better idea. The police couldn't question me if they couldn't find me. I hung up the phone and headed off to Hazel's to claim sanctuary.

Chapter Sixteen

Hazel would have made a great stop on the Underground Railroad. Sure, she would have died for the cause, but even more, she would have relished the intrigue. Showing up at her door at three in the morning with the threat of police pursuit was like handing her a birthday present.

She sat me at the kitchen table.

"I'll get us a snack. You show me what you got."

A snack? What I wanted was a tall Scotch, neat. Maybe a quart of it. There I was again, planning an escape into alcohol. What I got was hot chocolate soy milk with oatmeal cookies. Except for an occasional glass of wine over dinner with friends, Hazel doesn't drink. She's good with comfort foods though. I felt like a truant grade schooler. But grade schoolers don't often go to prison, so there was an upside. I would still have rather had the Scotch.

Cookies in hand, we settled into examining the papers. I'd come away with about half a ream, so maybe 250 pages. This was going to take some time. I took anything that looked financial since I had some knowledge of bookkeeping. Hazel took the correspondence and miscellanea. After an hour I'd had it. Nothing untoward had revealed itself, and the numbers were starting to look like stick cartoon characters walking across the page. I decided to turn in to better fight another day. I left Hazel sitting in the kitchen with her promise to *stash the loot* before going to bed herself. This woman was having way too much fun with my possible incarceration.

I stumbled into the kitchen next morning, running on barely three hours sleep. Hazel was still sitting at the table where I'd left her, reading through Shaw's papers. She didn't even have the good grace to look tired. She was as alert as a newly woken puppy with its favorite squeaky toy.

"Morning, Jo."

"Hey, Hazel. Had a fun night?"

"This man truly is appalling. I wouldn't exactly call reading his correspondence fun, but it is informative. Messenger isn't just a politician to him, Jo, she's a crusade. I don't know what he wouldn't do for her. It would be scary if it weren't so sad. Maybe it's both.

"But to get back on point, I didn't find any references to Rivera, Luis, or anyone else you mentioned as part of his group. There was one thing that caught my eye though. Here, look. This is the list of donors that you pulled out of his desk last night. Here is another list from the locked file drawer. They don't match. There are six names on the second list that don't show up on the first. I checked on the web earlier this morning, and sure enough the first list matches the reported contributors. The extra names are missing there too. Looks like there might be some campaign finance shenanigans, but what that might have to do with Rivera I don't know. Maybe one of these mystery contributors is Rivera by another name."

I leaned over her shoulder and looked at the second list. She had highlighted the questionable donors in neon yellow. The first name on the list jumped out at me like a slap in the face. But it had nothing to do with Rivera. At least not as far as I knew. ASP Inc.? That was Mark Miller's company. The Nordic-looking man with blue eyes and an overzealous handshake. Or, more to the immediate point, Latif's main man. The guy with the mandate to help find jobs and legal support for illegal immigrants. What possible reason could there be for him to be donating to Messenger's campaign? What was this? Was Messenger a closet supporter of immigration? I knew her politics better than to believe that. Maybe it was Mark who wasn't what he appeared to be. Could he be financing Messenger's anti-immigration campaign while pretending to be an advocate for immigration reform? But why would he? And, he and Latif were really tight. I couldn't imagine Latif as anything but the passionate advocate I'd come to like. Or, could I? I'd seen the rage and disgust in both men. If Mark was duplicitous, how could I trust my perception of Latif?

"What's the matter, Jo? You look like someone just dumped a bucket of ice water on your head."

"I've got to go Hazel. I need to look into something on this list. I'll check back with you later."

"If there's something suspicious on that list, Jo, you need to tell someone before you go digging in places where you might find trouble."

"It's nothing Hazel. Just a question I need to check into. I promise I won't chase any rabbits down holes until I'm sure there's no trap at the bottom. If you could keep looking through those papers, I'd appreciate it."

I turned and headed for the door, hoping to avoid further questions. It wasn't fair for me to show up on Hazel's doorstep in the wee hours of the morning, use her time and enthusiasm to slough through all those papers and then walk out without an explanation. But I wasn't about to tell her that Latif just walked into my crosshairs. She'd introduced us and they were good friends. Hazel is fiercely loyal. She wouldn't understand that I was so easily ready to doubt him. She would expect me to take his side, to believe in his innocence until proven guilty. But I'm not built like that. Trust doesn't come so easily to me. I can be as loyal as Hazel in the long run. But on the short track I'm prone to suspicion. It takes time for me to build up that kind of trust. And I hadn't known Latif nearly long enough.

I decided on the direct approach. Latif was one of those guys who shows up at work early and leaves late. I figured he should be in by now. I called his office. No answer. Next I called his department administrative assistant. Latif was out in the field today. No one who was around knew where he was or when he'd be in or even if he'd be in today.

I was way too agitated to let it rest a day. I hate even the hint of betrayal. I needed to know right then if he had been deceiving me. Besides, I still didn't know the fallout from my late night excursion. I'd avoided calling the office or home just in case someone was searching for me with an arrest warrant. If I didn't get to Latif today, I might not get the chance. By tomorrow I could be dodging questions in a police interrogation room.

I took myself to a late breakfast and then called Latif's office again. Still no answer, but I left a message telling him that we needed to talk and that I would be waiting in his lobby within the hour.

I headed over to the state office building, stopping at the library first, just long enough to pick up something to read during my wait. I didn't get past the first chapter before my phone rang.

"What do you mean, you're waiting in my lobby?"

"Well, hey there Latif. I need to talk with you and not over the phone."

"I have better things to do than drive back across town to meet with you. You are going to have to come up with a good reason for me to make the trip."

"Let's just say I have a good reason, a very good reason, one that you are going to want to hear. But I'm not talking about it here in the lobby."

"I'll meet you there in an hour. I tell you, Walker, this has been a rough week. I am not in the mood for being jerked around."

It was less than an hour before Latif showed up in the lobby looking like a bull aiming to flatten the idiot waving the pesky red cape in its face. We walked in silence to his office and took our places on opposite sides of his always cluttered desk.

Looking around his office again at all the pictures of his clients, I was finding it harder and harder to believe he could be involved in anything covert. I was feeling like a heel for even having imagined it. If I could have thought of a way to gracefully make an exit I would have been out of there. But I'd dragged Latif down here against his will. His glare would melt me to a puddle of plasma if I tried to back out now. He hadn't said a word, but just sat back in his chair waiting for me to give him a really good explanation for his return to the office.

I took the donor list from my pocket and unfolded it in front of him.

"What's this?" he asked, looking at me rather than at the list.

"A list of donors to Dorothea Messenger's campaign fund."

"And why do I care about it?"

"Just look at it."

I could see the moment he recognized Mark's company. It was the same moment I was absolutely convinced he knew nothing about the donations. His jaw clenched. His eyes narrowed.

"What is this, some kind of hoax? Are you trying to tell me that Mark Miller is making donations to Dorothea Messenger? That's absurd. Why would he do that?"

"That was my question for you. You've known him for a long time. Years, wasn't it? What's his connection to Messenger?"

"He doesn't have one. I'd swear to that. Who gave you this list?"

"I can't tell you that. But it came from Jacob Shaw's office."

"If you expect me to believe this, you're going to have to do better than that. I'm not going to trust an anonymous source that's likely got some hidden agenda."

Well not a hidden agenda, but certainly something to hide. I wasn't about to confess my crimes to a state employee, even if he was one of the good guys.

"I don't need you to trust anything. I just thought you might have an explanation."

"Like what, that Mark is working undercover for the state in some clandestine operation to gather information about Messenger? We don't work that way. Geez, Messenger is a U.S. Congresswoman. No one in this office has the clout to mess with her."

Too bad, I thought. I liked the idea of Mark as an undercover infiltrator a whole lot better than his being in cahoots with Messenger.

Latif shook his head.

"This must be some scheme of Shaw's to discredit Mark. Mark's been a real support for a lot of immigrants, legal and otherwise. Just the kind of man that Shaw would like to see brought down."

Maybe I should have left it there. But I knew he was wrong. Whatever else was true, this list hadn't been planted in a locked file cabinet in a locked office to discredit someone.

"That explanation doesn't wash, Latif. I can't tell you how I got the list, but it wasn't anywhere that Shaw could reasonably expect it to be circulated. This was no press release. I got it from someone who snuck it out of Shaw's office."

A lie, but a small one to keep the police at bay.

"And you don't think this person could have just been playing you?"

"No, not possible."

Latif stopped arguing. He wasn't convinced, but he was thinking on it. And I was doubting my decision to tell him. What if he confronted Mark? It wouldn't be hard to trace the list from Latif back to me and back to the unlocked doors at Messenger's office. Then another thought popped into my brain. Unrelated, but a question that I felt a sudden need to ask.

"By the way, Latif, when we met the first time, and I was asking you if you knew the dead girl, Angela, why didn't you mention the cell phone that Rosa says Angela had, with possibly incriminating pictures on it? They could be important."

He shook his big head.

"Could be important if they actually existed, which I have no way of knowing since I never saw the phone *or* the pictures. Rosa did tell me about that phone, after the fact, but I have no clue who or what was in those pictures, or why Angela might have believed they were important. That's not exactly evidence one can go to the police with."

I mulled that for a moment. It made sense, so I decided to drop it and return to the point at hand.

"Listen, Latif. It's really important that you not tell anyone about this. My source could be vulnerable." No doubt about that. I was feeling more vulnerable by the minute.

"I can't promise that. If Mark is giving this kind of money to Messenger I need to ask him why. But I won't tell him where I got the information."

I didn't like the sound of that, but I wasn't one of the people Latif felt obliged to listen to . . . now more than ever. Maybe I could get Hazel to ask him to back off. I didn't need him getting in the middle of this story and raising alarms with Mark or Messenger's crowd before I could figure what was going on.

"Will you at least call me to let me know what Mark has to say?"

"Maybe. I suppose it depends on what he says. I'm not forgetting that you work for the press. I'm not looking to set Mark up for a headline in your paper. If I think it's anything you need to know, I'll give you a call."

With that unsatisfactory resolution I left Latif's office. Time to go home and find out if there were police parked on my doorstep.

On my way I called Hazel to fill her in on my talk with Latif, skipping the part about my earlier suspicions about him. Her news was not good.

"Linda called a little while ago. The police showed up at her office this morning looking for you. Of course she told them everything. That you hadn't been home when she woke up this morning. That she hadn't been able to reach you at work. I don't know what to do with that girl. She'd inform on her own daughter for breaking a law even for the best of causes."

"She gets that from you, Hazel. Moral certitude. You just serve different masters."

I could have predicted Linda's response. She takes her position as an officer of the court very seriously. I should have called her first thing in the morning. Then she would have been thinking of me as a client and all the forces of the universe wouldn't have been able to drag a word from her. I needed to call her immediately to get her firmly in my camp.

I pulled to the side of the road to place the call. No point adding an accident to the complication my life was becoming. This conversation was likely to take all my concentration.

Linda's secretary, Debbie, put my call right through. Not a good sign. Usually Debbie makes me run a gauntlet before being allowed an audience with the Queen. She doesn't like me much. She thinks I'm too much of a loose cannon. But she and Linda are a perfect match. They both like their lives orderly and predictable. Which begs the question of why Linda has me for a roommate. But then she was raised by a woman with the potential disruptive force of a hurricane, so she was somewhat acclimated.

Before I could even say hello, Linda blurted out, "Tell me you didn't break into Messenger's office last night."

"Wish I could."

"Jo, what were you thinking?"

"I was thinking I have the best lawyer in the state of Colorado."

Linda isn't at all susceptible to flattery. I was just hoping at this point that she would agree that she was my lawyer.

"Well I'm glad to hear you think so. You may need a good lawyer soon. The FBI showed up in my office this morning looking for you."

"The FBI?" I think my voice actually squeaked.

"Messenger is a U.S. congresswoman. Who did you think would investigate a break-in at her office?"

"Hazel said it was the police."

"I told her that because I didn't want her saddling up her white charger and galloping into the fray. We need to keep this situation low key. The last thing we want is for the FBI to think we're throwing down a challenge."

Sometimes even I have to admit that I don't always think things through as completely as I might. This was one of those times. I was wishing I was sitting in Linda's office so I could give her a doleful, puppy dog look. You'd think a high-powered lawyer like Linda wouldn't be susceptible to such overt manipulation. But that's another trait she shares with Hazel: neither one of them can abandon a helpless creature stranded on the roadside. I figured I was in dire need of some of that compassion right now.

Luckily, Linda and I have been friends forever. She doesn't need to see me to know when I'm feeling desperate for a rescue. And she has never abandoned me.

I could hear the sigh in her voice.

"The FBI agent left a business card. I'll call and set up a meeting in my office later today if I can arrange it. You disappear for a few hours. Don't go home, don't go to my mother's and don't go to the office. Better that I make first contact than that they find you on their own. I'll call when I have a time. Meanwhile, you need to call *The Review*. I'm sure the FBI has called there looking for you. If I know Ed, he's circled the troops and is ready for Custer's Last Stand in your defense. Don't let that happen. Just for once, try to keep it simple."

With that she was gone.

I'm not sure how she expected to keep breaking-and-entering simple. But she was right that *The Review* was probably in an uproar by now. If I called in, Ed would insist that I return to the office where I could very well expect to be sequestered in a hidden bunker, guarded by snarling reporters and their guard dogs. Since the only dogs residing with *The Review* staff were a Cocker Spaniel, a couple of Golden Retrievers, and one miniature Poodle, the dogs weren't all that intimidating. But reporters can be downright mean. In any case, if I was going to meet with Linda and the FBI later, it would be impossible to extricate myself from the tentacles of all that outraged zeal. Ed was pretty level-headed, but his wife Annie might well already be planning a siege of the FBI building for my rescue. Not surprisingly, she and Hazel were best friends.

I decided my best course of action was avoidance. I called Hazel and asked her to contact Ed and Annie for me. I figured they could plan my escape to Canada while I hid out. With that taken care of, I headed off to the Denver Zoo for a day of hiding among the saner animals of our planet.

Chapter Seventeen

I showed up at Linda's office at 4:00 p.m., my toothbrush, a clean set of underwear, and a box lunch stuffed in my bag. I figured if I was arrested at least I'd be clean and well fed for a day.

The meeting was formal. We sat in a conference room.

Linda and I on one side of the long table, two FBI agents facing us. They were mixed gender. The guy looked barely old enough to be through puberty. He sat ramrod straight with a stare that seemed to look right through me. If that stare was intended to intimidate me, it missed its mark. The guy hadn't said a word and already I was feeling like challenging him to a duel. The woman was old enough to be his mother but didn't look as if a maternal thought had ever crossed her mind.

Linda's chair sat snug up against mine, which might have been interpreted by the agents as a protective stance. But we both knew she had strategically positioned herself to kick my shins if I started getting out of line. It was a serious risk. I'd learned at Hazel's knee to distrust authority and to start snarling as soon as they showed any sign of disrespect. My hackles were already rising.

The young guy, whose name I'd immediately forgotten, started the interrogation. "Ms. Walker can you tell us where you were last night from 10:00 p.m. until 6:00 a.m. this morning?"

"Maybe. Why do you want to know?"

"Please just answer the question."

"You first."

He shifted in his chair and frowned. Here was a guy who liked to be in control. I revised my age estimate to include a stint in the military, probably an officer. He looked at his companion, who gave a slight nod.

"We're investigating a possible break-in at Congresswoman Messenger's office last night. The security guard reported that your car was in the parking lot when he made his rounds. Can you explain that?"

"I was in bed most of the night."

"What?"

"You asked me what I was doing last night. I was home in bed."

"Can someone verify that?"

"No, I don't think so. Well, maybe Bosco." A smack from Linda's foot told me I was on the verge of going home lame tonight.

"Bosco?"

"The family dog. He's very smart, a Border Collie. He compulsively keeps track of everyone in his house. I'm sure he knew I was home." This was kind of fun. I might even be enjoying this interview if Linda wasn't using my leg for kick boxing practice.

"You know, Ms. Walker, this isn't a joke. You are in serious trouble."

"And why is that? Are you accusing me of something?"

He paused and took a deep breath. "Can you explain why your car was at Congresswoman Messenger's office?"

"I'm not going to answer any questions until you tell me your reasons for asking them. If you suspect I committed a crime, I want to know it now."

"And is that because you have something to hide?" he blurted out. His cool was definitely on the slide. I had him off balance and was loving it. Maybe I should spend more time chatting with the

FBI. Although, I suspected I was dealing with the new kid on the block, not the A team.

"No, I'm just a big fan of my civil rights. I'd like to keep them around for a while."

His female companion interceded.

"This is just an interview to gather some facts. We are not accusing you of anything. We would appreciate your cooperation, Ms. Walker."

"I was at Messenger's office yesterday and when I left, my car wouldn't start, so I left it there."

"But it wasn't there this morning."

"A friend and I went to pick it up early so I'd have it for work today." It was the story Hazel and I had plotted out last night.

"And what time was that?"

"I'm not sure. 2:00, 3:00 a.m., something like that."

The agents looked at each other. I was in the right time frame, I knew that. But they couldn't tell if that was because I was telling the truth, or because I knew the time of the break-in because I'd committed it.

"An odd time to pick up a car, isn't it?" she said.

"What can I say? We're odd people."

"And who is this friend who picked up the car with you."

This was a bit awkward. Linda was not going to be happy with me for dragging her mother into this lie. I gave them Hazel's name and phone number, daring a glance in Linda's direction. She just gave a barely visible shake of her head. Hazel and I getting into trouble together was nothing new to Linda.

The FBI wasn't quite through with me yet. The guy took up the questioning again. Bad strategy. I was liking him less by the minute.

"What were you doing at Messenger's office yesterday?"

"I'm a newspaper reporter. I wanted to interview Jacob Shaw for a story, but I couldn't get in to see him."

"He refused to see you?"

"That's right. Guess he had other plans." A knowing smile made me suspect he'd found a motive. Revenge for a snubbed reception. Really, I thought. If that were the case, I'd spend my life breaking into government buildings, factories and an occasional grade school.

"What was the story you wanted to talk with him about?"

"That's not your business."

The guy almost snarled. Clearly they'd let him out on the street way too green if I could ruffle his feathers this easily.

"Information about anything that might endanger Congresswoman Messenger is my business."

I was starting to feel pretty hot under the collar myself.

"I didn't do anything to endanger the congresswoman. If you want information on my story, you'll have to take it up with my newspaper."

Ed would eat this guy for lunch and enjoy every bite. I reached for my phone. Now seemed like as good a time as any to get that meal started. Linda reached for my hand at the same time the woman agent spoke out.

"Let's not get ahead of ourselves. We'll check out what you've told us, and if we have any more questions, we'll contact you. In the meantime," she said, standing, "if you have anything you'd like to add to your statement, here's my card. Just call."

I hadn't convinced either of them of my explanation. Not surprising since it wasn't true. But at least I wasn't going to be spending the night in jail.

Chapter Eighteen

As soon as I left Linda's office, I placed a call to Hazel warning her that the FBI could be showing up on her doorstep any minute, or tapping her phones, or whatever they do to snag miscreants like me. I could almost see her smiling and gleefully rubbing her hands. She was having way too much fun at my expense.

Next I called *The Review* office. Ed was in an uproar. He demanded that I give an accounting of myself in person at the office, while promising to defend me from the FBI with lawsuits, threats, capitol-step rallies, and by putting his body in front of mine, if it came to that. I sure hoped someone was keeping track of his blood pressure.

Begging debilitating fatigue from battling the foes of the free press, I finally got him to agree to delay until morning what looked to be another interrogation.

"If you want to help me, Ed, could you do a background check on Mark Miller?"

"Miller? You mean the guy who's working with the anti-trafficking committee? What's he got to do with this?"

"Ask me questions tomorrow. For now can you just dig around and see if any dirt surfaces?"

"I'll get someone on it but I'll expect you to be ready with some good answers tomorrow."

With that not so subtle threat echoing in my head, I climbed into my car and headed downtown. I had lied to Ed. I wasn't actually tired in the least. I was wound up like a jack-in-the-box waiting for someone to pop the spring. I needed answers a lot more than I needed rest. My first step was to figure out the connection between Mark Miller and Jacob Shaw. There was something fishy there.

My call to Latif was answered by his voice mail. But I knew where I'd be able to find both Mark and Latif. It was Wednesday night, and the Colorado Anti-Trafficking Committee would meet at the state office building in a couple of hours.

I had decided that in the interim a clandestine visit to Mark's hotel might be revealing. I wasn't planning another break-in, but if an opportunity to get into his office presented itself, well, I'd brought along my lock picks just in case.

Heading to the hotel, I wondered idly what was happening to my morals. The thought of a second break-in within 24 hours wasn't bothering me in the least. Maybe I was becoming an adrenaline junkie. Or maybe I just really hated being lied to. I needed to find out the truth of what was going on. I may not be an adrenaline junkie, but a truth junkie. I have zero tolerance for unanswered questions. I couldn't make crime my research method of choice. But all my moral doubts were a waste of energy and I knew it. No amount of self-flagellation was going to stop me. So off to the hotel I went.

I parked downtown on 17th Street and walked the few blocks to the Carlton. The lobby was full of people . . . checking in, waiting for taxis, and sitting around reading newspapers. When I asked for Mark's office, I was pointed to a door behind the registration desk and informed that he had already left for dinner. There was no chance I would make this a two-crime spree, not with the desk fully staffed.

The desk clerk told me that Mark usually dined in the hotel

restaurant on nights he stayed in town. I decided to check that he was in the early stages of his meal so I could be sure he was occupied. I still hoped to pull off an unapproved tour of the hotel.

I worked my way to the restaurant doors and peeked around the corner. Mark and Latif were seated at a window table. So, I thought, Latif had decided to confront Mark with the information I'd brought him this morning. Or, I assumed that was the reason for their meeting. I just hoped Latif kept his promise to leave me out of the conversation. I didn't want to explain how I'd gotten the list. In any case, the appetizers were still sitting on the table, so I would have time for a bit of reconnaissance.

I had no idea what I was looking for, so I had no idea where to start. I had some vague theory that Mark might be supporting Messenger because he could get cheaper labor from tougher immigration laws. It made a kind of sense. People threatened with tougher laws could be paid less, treated worse, and be manipulated more easily. No unions or living wages for these folks. I couldn't get to pay records, which would probably be doctored anyhow, but I could check out the working conditions at the hotel.

I went to the reception desk and asked for a map of the hotel, claiming an interest in the facilities for a weekend romantic retreat. The guy at the desk was chatty, and mildly flirtatious, leaning in too close and batting his eyelashes like a teenager. If I had really wanted a romantic outing I could have taken him upstairs right then. But he was ten years too young and too clean cut for my taste. Still, by the time I walked away I knew the location of every nook and cranny in the hotel, including where to find the housekeeping staff.

Map in hand I headed off to one of the rooms marked for "Staff Use," which my informant had assured me was the laundry and staff lockers. Not surprisingly it was locked by a mechanism that required a key card. This was well beyond my breaking and entering abilities. I walked back down to the lobby and placed a call to housekeeping, requesting clean towels for room 620, a completely arbitrary choice. I sprinted back to housekeeping and arrived just as a maid in a starched black uniform was exiting the room. She didn't look back and I was able to catch the door behind her just before it latched.

No one looked up as I entered. The room was almost empty. Most of the guest rooms would have been cleaned and the work done long ago. This was just a skeleton staff left to answer guest requests through the evening and night. The few women in the room seemed to be finishing up the laundry. They were folding sheets, talking in soft voices. There was the settled feeling of a day winding down.

I passed through the laundry and entered a room lined with lockers. Not a thumb screw, rack, or whip in sight. I was feeling dumber by the minute. How exactly was I going to recognize employee abuse if I saw it? I left the locker room and exited the laundry without having exchanged a word with the women working there.

Further down the hall was another room marked on the map for "Staff Use". This one bore the sign, "No Admittance." I was feeling foolish and ready to go hunt up dinner, but this door had a regular lock, no key card admittance here. Probably a storage room, but it might be worth a look.

It was no storage room. As I leaned close to the door and pulled my lock picks from my pocket, I could hear a television and a man yelling. Suddenly it didn't seem like such a good idea to open that door. Still, if I could just get a peek at what was going on, I might learn something interesting.

It took me somewhat less than ten minutes to pick the lock. I was getting better at this all the time. I turned the doorknob slowly and cracked the door open. Two men were sitting with their backs to me watching a baseball game. The yelling was aimed at the television, where the manager of the Colorado Rockies was berating an umpire. Clearly the men agreed with the manager.

My view of the rest of the room was blocked by the door. I opened it wider and stuck my head through the opening. Four young women sat on a couch, huddled together like puppies. Not one of them looked old enough to get a driver's license. They wore skirts that would barely have covered their butts if they stood up and flimsy blouses that suggested more than they hid. I had no doubt about how these girls made money and less doubt about the purpose of the men who sat guard. So, Mark wanted to purify the reputation of the hospitality industry of the taint of prostitution. Looked to me like he was providing the service.

One of the girls turned her head and stared right at me. The right side of her face was bruised and swollen. Her hands, which I had thought were folded in her lap, were bound with cord and tied to the couch. It took every ounce of will to stop myself from charging into that room and dragging all four of them out. But what I needed to do was get to a phone and call the police without alerting the men that I had been here. I was hardly a match for these two guys, even in a fit of rage.

I started pulling back from the door. But as I moved, the injured girl let out a sob. It must have looked as if I were abandoning her there. At the sound, both men looked up and followed her stare to see me standing in the doorway. They both charged at me as I slammed the door in their faces.

This was way more than I was prepared for. My only chance was to make it back to the public areas of the hotel. I ran through the corridors and sprinted into the lobby with only a few feet lead. They fell back as I approached the main desk. My friend was still staffing the desk.

"Call the police."

"Why, what's happened?"

"Just call them."

He picked up the receiver but didn't place a call. One of the men had taken a seat in the lobby and was watching me.

The other had disappeared. I had to get the police here right away before the missing man moved the girls to a different location.

I grabbed the phone and started punching buttons, trying to connect to an outside line. I got through, yelling to the dispatcher that a woman's life was in danger. After I'd extracted a promise for immediate help, I hung up and handed the map to the desk clerk who was standing slack jawed, staring at me.

"When the police get here, send them to this room," I said, pointing to the area where I'd seen the girls.

When he didn't respond I grabbed a pen, marked the map with a big X and shoved it back in his hand.

"There, got it?"

"Yeah, sure."

With that meager confirmation I ran back to the room.

I didn't know how, but I had to keep the girls in that room until the police arrived.

When I got to the room, the door was wide open. It was deserted. I think I actually screamed out loud, though I don't remember what I was yelling. I started running up and down the hallways looking for any sign of where they might have been taken. But the hotel had hundreds of rooms. They could be in any of them, or even, and more likely, in the back of a van driving away at this minute. I sat down in the middle of the hallway and started pounding the floor.

It was awhile before I had calmed down enough to start thinking again. I had to get out of here. I had nothing to give the police that I hadn't already told the dispatcher. And if I waited to be questioned, Mark would find out that I was the person who had entered the room. One of his men had gotten a good look at me when I called the police from the reception desk. But Mark might not make the connection just from the description if I was able to avoid a police interview. And if I could let Mark keep up his facade, I had a better chance of figuring out what was going on with him and Messenger.

I exited the hotel through a side door, carefully avoiding dark corners until I made my way to my car. As I pulled away I realized that I had never questioned whether the men who had chased me in the hotel worked for Mark. I had just assumed it. And, though I had no proof and no real reason, I still believed it. There were too many coincidences spinning around the man. I needed to talk to Latif. He was the one person I could think of who might be able to help me figure this out.

Chapter Nineteen

I went directly from the hotel to the state office building where the Colorado Anti-Trafficking Committee would be meeting at 8:00. I was an hour early because I had already decided that I was going to skip the meeting. After the near fiasco at the hotel, it didn't seem like a good idea to meet face to face with Mark. He might have realized I was the person who'd seen the prostitutes. Even if he didn't, I wasn't sure I could control my anger if I saw him.

Still, I needed to check with Latif. I wanted to hear about his dinner conversation with Mark, and I wanted his advice on what I should do about what I'd seen at the hotel.

My plan was to wait outside the state office building until Latif showed up. He ran the meeting and so would presumably be there early.

I could at least grab enough of his time to tell him what I'd seen and arrange a meeting for later that night.

I sat back in my car, pulled out a flashlight and book, and settled in for a read. As 8:00 p.m. approached, I watched the different committee members arrive. But no sign of Latif. Maybe the meeting with Mark had run over. By 8:30 Latif still hadn't arrived, and I was getting worried.

At 8:45 Mark walked by. I ducked low in the car, but he appeared not to notice me and headed directly into the building. There was still no sign of Latif. By 9:00 everyone headed back out to their cars. Marianne Boxer, whom I'd met at Latif's office, was the last to exit. I left my car and ran up to her. Her immediate assumption was that I was late to arrive for the meeting.

"Hi, Ms. Walker," she said. "Looks like there's no meeting tonight. Latif never showed up and there was no point in having the meeting without him."

"Strange that he didn't show up. Any idea what happened? Did he call anyone before the meeting with an explanation?"

"No, just a no-show. I hope nothing's wrong. With his job an emergency can come up at any time. Still, it's the first time I've known him to miss this meeting."

"I saw Mark Miller go in. I know Latif had planned to have dinner with him tonight. Did he have an explanation?"

Marianne scowled briefly.

"Mark said he hadn't spoken to Latif today. Their dinner plans must have gotten canceled. Still, you'd think Latif must have given him some explanation for canceling. But, no, Mark was as confused as the rest of us."

I didn't know why Mark was lying. But I wasn't going to get into that with Marianne.

"Well, I'm concerned. I've left a couple of messages on his phone, but he hasn't responded. Any idea how I might reach him?"

"Afraid not. But if you do find him, will you give me a call? Now you've got me worried too."

After mutual assurances that we were both just alarmists, Marianne headed back to her car and I headed back to my phone. I didn't think I was an alarmist. Something wasn't right. I could feel it in my gut.

Hazel wasn't home, but I left a message asking for a call back with some alternate way to contact Latif. Then I headed off in search of an internet connection to see if I could locate Latif's home address.

I was working my way through every address site on the web with no success when Hazel called at 10:00. Apparently Latif was very protective of his privacy and very successful at keeping it hidden, which was just plain good sense with his job. But Hazel was a friend and had been to his house frequently. She was willing to share the location, but on the condition that she accompany me.

Having Hazel along on the search wasn't my first choice. Hazel is great company, but she can make a trip to the grocery store for a gallon of ice cream seem like an expedition to the North Pole in search of the abominable snowman. The world isn't simple to Hazel and she infuses complexity into her every action. It makes life interesting, but it can be a lot of work being with Hazel and I was hoping to be in bed before sunrise. After all, I'd been up until the wee hours last night breaking into an office building. It had been an insanely long day. It seemed like I deserved some rest from my labors. Still, if something was wrong, I'd trust Hazel's instincts over anyone else, including my own. So, having her company might not be such a bad idea. Within a half hour I'd picked her up and we were heading east toward Aurora.

On the ride over I told Hazel about my visit to Mark's hotel. She was predictably outraged. Less predictably, she wanted me to go directly to the police. I refused. I'd already called the police and if there was anything they could do, it was already being done.

"Jo, you can't just walk away from this and leave the police to investigate on their own," she argued. "You need to talk with them. Find out what they're doing about it. Make sure they make it a priority."

Okay, this was sounding more like the Hazel I knew. One of her mottoes, and she has many, is that you're personally responsible to take action against any injustice you witness. No handing it off to the police, social workers, or God's will. But at the moment I was more concerned about Latif than police efficiency.

Besides, I had to stay under the radar on this one. If I was publicly connected to the police investigation, all chance of my discovering the truth would just evaporate.

"Hazel, I just can't get involved in that way. If Mark or Rivera find out what I know, they'll never talk to me again. I need access to figure out what is going on."

Hazel gave me a disgusted look. "The fate of the girls caught up in this racket is a whole lot more important than your story, Jo."

That hurt. It wasn't like Hazel to doubt my motives.

She knew me better than that.

"It's not the story. You know that. The police are looking at an isolated crime. There's a lot more going on here. What about Mark's contribution to Messenger's campaign? And the murdered girl? Nailing Mark for pimping or even for holding the girls against their will isn't enough. We need the whole picture."

Hazel didn't relent. Finally we agreed that after we found Latif she would call Cap. He could find out what the police were doing. If he thought my testimony was critical to the police investigation, then Hazel and I could pick up our argument. But I extracted her promise that she wouldn't tell Cap anything until he agreed not to involve me without my consent. I felt like someone had lit a fuse under me. I'd better work fast before all the people I was keeping secrets from got together and came after me.

Latif lived in a small ranch style house on a quiet street not far from the town center of Aurora. It wasn't so quiet tonight. Latif's two Pugs were jumping at the back fence barking and wagging their little tails. Other than that there was no sign of life. The house was dark. There was no car in the driveway.

"Well that's not right," Hazel said. "Latif never leaves the dogs out at night. They make too much racket, like they're doing now. He always locks their dog door and keeps them in after he feeds them their dinner."

The dogs' excitement at being left out in the forbidden night was clearly accompanied by anxiety. Whines were mixed with their barks, and they followed us as we walked along the fence line like, well, lost puppies. I wondered if Latif had even gotten home to give them their dinner. Hazel clearly was wondering the same thing.

"Well this won't do, will it?" she said, addressing the dogs. She reached over the fence and released the latch. Both dogs charged Hazel as I stepped through into the backyard.

While Hazel dealt with the canines, I walked around the back of the house, peering through windows. There wasn't much to see. It was pitch black inside and there was no sound of a television or radio. Knowing Latif, I wouldn't have been surprised if he didn't even own a television. But there was no other indication that anyone was home. It was after 10:30 on a work night. Latif wasn't exactly a party animal. As far as I could surmise, he should have been here. And he certainly wouldn't have just left the dogs out to annoy the neighbors, even if he had a late appointment. Something serious must have happened to divert him from both the committee meeting and his canine responsibility. I just wished he would answer his phone so I'd know what was going on.

My lock picks were still in the car. I considered breaking into his house to see if I could find any clues as to his whereabouts. But this wasn't an enemy camp. This was a friend's house. Latif would not forgive the breach of privacy if he found out. Besides, Hazel would never allow it. She had found a rope somewhere, had tied both dogs to a fence post and was walking in my direction.

We both walked around the house peering into the same windows I'd already tried. We tested the doors to see if any would open. No success. After a few more half-hearted attempts to gain entry, we decided it was time to leave, before the neighbors noticed and reported an attempted break-in. That would be the perfect ending to my day. Besides, there was nothing more that we could do.

Hazel wrote a note to Latif, posted it on the front door and loaded the two Pugs into my car. I wasn't particularly happy with that arrangement. I knew where the dogs would be spending the night. Hazel's cat, Emily, would never allow two such rambunctious intruders into her domain. There'd be shredded Pugs by morning. Whereas Bosco would love a couple of new friends for a slumber party.

On the drive home Hazel called Cap and gave him the whole story of my visit to the hotel and our search for Latif. Generously she omitted the details of how I gained entry to the room where I saw the girls. I heard Hazel state my demand for anonymity, but I didn't hear Cap agree to it. Cap is a kind of by-the-rules guy. Which does beg the question of what he is doing with Hazel. I couldn't see him agreeing to keep any information from his former colleagues at the police department. I could only hope they would keep my name confidential if it came to that.

But Cap wasn't easy to convince. He wanted me to call the police myself. As Hazel relayed, he thought it was too serious a crime for him to play armchair quarterback. Since retiring from the police force, Cap didn't like to get too involved with police business. An occasional consult was all he was willing to accept. But with Hazel as his main squeeze, his attempts were doomed. Hazel doesn't understand non-involvement. And has no patience with it in others.

By the time we reached Hazel's house, Cap had agreed to a breakfast meeting the next morning. Oh good, I thought, one more person to equivocate with. It was getting hard to keep track of who I'd told what. I needed someone I could tell the whole story to, someone who could help me clear my head without trying to force my hand. I decided that after breakfast in the morning it was time for a visit to *The Review* and a long chat with my editor.

After dropping Hazel off I headed home in search of kibble and a couple of beds for my two passengers, who were snoring loudly in the back seat. I could hardly wait to see Latif's face when he found out his pups had spent the night in my care. At this point I'd be happy to see his face even if it was snarling at me.

Chapter Twenty

I didn't sleep well that night. As I'd predicted, Bosco was more than happy to have company. That's a marvelous thing about most dogs: they make friends more easily than water runs downhill. After the normal butt–sniff greetings, they were off to play. The new friendship got rowdy fast. An hour of tag, leap and bark, and we human residents were ready to do some barking of our own. Luckily dogs didn't outnumber people in the house.

With Linda restraining Bosco, Jessie and I each grabbed a Pug and headed to my bedroom.

Sharing a room with them didn't make for a restful night. When the dogs weren't scratching at the door and whining, their snoring was enough to seriously annoy the dead. Which left me with my pillow stuffed in my ears, tossing through the night. Latif was going to owe me one for this.

Even the prospect of pancakes at my favorite diner wasn't enough to snap me out of my sulk next morning. Hazel was sitting beside Cap when I walked in for breakfast. That was good. I could use the moral support. Of course, she had her own reasons for being there. Hazel wasn't going to sit back and take in the scenery when Latif might be in danger.

She was dressed in a gray linen suit and looked as prim as a preacher's wife. Or, the picture I have of preachers' wives from reruns of 1960s television shows. I'm always impressed but never fooled by Hazel's disguises. I wondered how much of it Cap bought. He was a practical, down-to-earth kind of guy. Still, if he found Hazel with her hand in the proverbial cookie jar, he'd assume she was putting cookies in, probably for starving children. If blindness was any measure of love, Cap was head over heels with Hazel.

His blindness didn't extend to me, though. He examined me with the steady, unyielding manner of the police captain he had been. If the FBI guys had looked at me that way, I would have confessed to the Messenger break-in and every other crime I'd committed since stealing candy in grade school.

Confrontation I'm good at. I love a good fight. But the silent treatment gets me every time. Silence is a vacuum. It begs to be filled with answers, answers to the questions nobody is asking. Of course, the trick is to answer the right unasked question so you're not giving away more information than necessary.

"Morning, Jo," Cap said.

"Hey, Cap. How's things?"

"Good, you?"

"Good."

"So, have you given any more thought to what I said last night?"

Straight to the point. That was another thing to like about Cap. I decided to follow his example.

"Cap, I just can't go to the police with this. I don't have enough information. It wouldn't be hard for someone to explain away what I saw. It's not like I took pictures."

"Well, from what Hazel told me there's good reason for suspicion. You can at least tell the police what you do know. It might help them be prepared if something comes up."

I had to admit that sounded reasonable. If only so much of what I knew hadn't been obtained illegally. I looked to Hazel for help. She might as well have been in a different room for all the interest she was showing in this conversation. So much for moral support. She'd insisted I call in Cap, and now was watching me squirm in front of him. I was on my own here.

After that, breakfast proceeded rather as I had expected. Cap wanted me to go to the police. I refused. Cap wanted to know where I'd gotten the list of Messenger's donors. I equivocated. Cap wanted to know if I'd happened to find the list by breaking into Messenger's office. I lied. Before breakfast arrived at the table, he was ready to slap me in handcuffs and march me down to police headquarters just on general principle. The pancakes in front of me were losing their appeal. There wasn't a stack of pancakes tall enough to bridge the gap between what I was willing to do and what Cap wanted from me.

When Cap finally resigned himself to the fact that I wasn't going to play the part of a responsible, reasonable citizen, I was able to glean some information. At his request the police had checked out Latif's house and work.

"There was no sign of him at his house. No sign of a break-in either. Just one neighbor who reported seeing a couple of strangers sniffing around the house around midnight peering in windows and such. I expect that was you gals. The neighbor didn't report it: he figured it must be friends since the dogs stopped their racket."

Well they didn't exactly stop the racket, they just moved it to my house. But I figured Cap was right . . . it probably was us. So much for Hazel and I starting careers as cat burglars.

"Latif didn't show up for work this morning either. He had clients scheduled, but when they arrived he still hadn't come in. That's got folks at his office worried. They contacted some of his family—apparently he's got a sister in town—but no one's heard from him."

"There must be something wrong Cap. Latif might blow off a committee meeting," though even that was hard to imagine, "but he would never skip out on one of his clients. Some of them hang on by a thread, and he's the thread. He wouldn't disappoint them."

Cap scowled at me.

"That would be a good reason for you to think about talking with the police."

I didn't want to start up that argument again. It wasn't going to happen. Not till I had something more concrete to say.

When I didn't respond, Cap continued his report.

"The last person to see Latif, that the police could find, was another social worker at the agency. She walked by his office around 8:30 p.m. and heard him yelling over the phone. She said that was so unlike Latif, she decided she'd better check to see if he was okay. When she poked her head in his office, he just shook his head and waved her off. She didn't like that response much, but decided to let it ride. I guess she wishes now that she'd stayed to ask a few questions."

"Did she remember any of what he said?"

"Not specifically. She had thought maybe he just finally reached his limit with one of his clients because he said things like he wasn't going to listen to any more lies, he wanted to know what had really happened, that kind of thing. Other than that, she had no idea who he was talking with. She was on her way out so she didn't know when he left."

I kind of wished she'd stayed around to ask more questions too. At least this meant he had been okay after meeting with Mark. For that matter, Mark had arrived at the committee meeting shortly after the woman had seen Latif at the office.

Did that let Mark off the hook for Latif's disappearance? Or did it simply make it all the more clear that Mark was indeed involved?

One thing was certain: something about that phone call had made Latif blow off the committee meeting. That call had taken him somewhere else, and he hadn't been seen since.

My gut was telling me what my next move needed to be, and that knowledge was going to make it pretty tough to digest my pancakes.

Chapter Twenty-One

At 8 p.m. downtown Denver is a pretty lively place, even on a weeknight. I parked in a lot on Market Street and joined the people walking along the 16th Street Mall, heading south. I'd spent the entire afternoon contemplating what I wanted to say to Mark Miller, and I still hadn't decided on a firm plan of action. I couldn't just barge into his office at the Carlton Hotel demanding to know what he'd done to Latif. Well, I could, and it would be right in line with my normal behavior. But, my normal behavior wasn't getting me very far yet. I needed a different approach . . . one with finesse. I'm not good with finesse, especially when I'm angry.

When I walked into the lobby, Mark was standing at the front desk talking to a woman who appeared to be a hotel guest. I walked up behind the woman so that I would be in his line of sight, but didn't interrupt the conversation. It was idle chit chat. Mark was talking about the city. Good places to dine, the latest exhibit at the art museum, the art galleries on South Santa Fe. His gentle laugh had the woman smiling. As he talked, he walked her to the exit and with a slight bow opened the door, while signaling a porter to grab a cab for her.

Then he turned and looked back at me. Gone was the charm, the laughter. His eyes were flat, his face expressionless. Who could do that, turn off emotion like a switch?

He grabbed my elbow, pulling me past the reception desk.

There was no way I was going anywhere with this man. I pulled away, but his grasp was like a vice.

"Let go of me or I am going to start screaming," I said.

He paused. "I think this conversation requires some privacy."

I looked around, pulled my arm away from him and walked to a deserted waiting area that was still in view of the reception desk. He followed. I sat, putting a small table between us. He didn't sit.

"What have you done to Latif?" So much for finesse.

He didn't answer.

"Look, I saw you two together before he disappeared, here having dinner. And I know you've got some kind of deal going with Messenger. I told Latif. He came here to talk with you about it and then he vanished. So, where is he?"

"Let me be clear about this, Walker. Stay out of my business."

It would have been a good time to shut up. This man was potentially dangerous and I didn't want to be in his sights. Still....

"Or what? I'm not a scared little girl from Mexico that you can cow with threats. And, I've been to the police. Anything happens to me and you are on the hot seat."

Well, I hadn't actually been to the police, unless a retired Captain counts. But I thought it sounded good.

"You've had your warning, Walker. That's all you get," he hissed, and walked away.

I left the hotel and headed back down 16th Street toward my car, feeling completely creeped out. I couldn't believe that I had once thought Mark might be a good man. God, it was scary. Either my judgment was totally off base, or he deserved an Oscar. Either way, I was way more frightened for Latif than I'd been when I walked in the hotel. Was Mark really responsible for his disappearance? I just couldn't think about it. I felt that the man might be capable of anything.

Now where? The whole thing with Mark hadn't taken an hour.

Still, I couldn't think of anything else to do this late. I decided I'd just have to wait until morning. Maybe sleep would knock some brain cells loose and I'd come up with a masterful plan by breakfast.

I drove across town, heading for home, trying to come up with what I was going to say to Linda if she asked what I'd been up to. I suppose I could just drive around town for a couple of hours until she'd gone to bed and then sneak into the house unnoticed. But I was just too tired. And the conversation with Mark had been the final straw. I wanted my bed and I wanted it now. I'd have to convince Linda to wait until morning for any lectures.

The lights were still on in the family room when I pulled into the driveway. I opened the car door, stepped out and could distantly hear the television. So, that meant Linda and Jessie were both still up. Since Linda rarely watched TV, she must be in the office on the other side of the house.

When I went around the 4Runner to get my stuff from the rear, something hit me hard across the back of my head. I saw a flash of white light and fell to the concrete driveway. I must have blacked out. I came to aware that someone had pulled duct tape over my mouth and was putting a sack over my body. It fell down to my legs and smelled like dirty laundry. I tried to pull away. My arms were tugged behind my back.

Something was holding them, something metal . . . handcuffs. All I could do was start kicking. But, with my head spinning from the blow, and wrapped in a laundry sack, I couldn't even find anything to kick. I felt someone grab my legs. More duct tape, this time around my ankles. I couldn't scream or kick. All I could do was squirm. That was getting me nowhere. I had to find a way to signal Linda or Jessie that I was in trouble so they would call the police. Or, did I? What if they just came out to investigate? I didn't want them to meet these thugs. I stopped struggling and let them pick me up like a log, someone at my feet, and my shoulders jammed under someone's armpit. They must have carried me back down the driveway. I heard a car door open.

"Get her in the trunk, quick. This is no place to stand around. Move it."

With a grunt someone lifted me and wedged me into a small space without enough room to even straighten my legs. So, not a Cadillac, I thought. Then I heard a thump and the trunk hood closed over me. The car started and pulled out on the street. I could feel the car accelerating to highway speed.

It was hard to tell time. I couldn't decide if I had blacked out again or if I was just too muddleheaded to track what was going on. I knew at some level I must be afraid, terrified, but my head ached like a thousand migraines and I just couldn't hold a thought. Even terror seemed out of reach. After some undefined time had passed, the car hit a dirt road, drove awhile longer and then stopped. There was more banging of doors. Someone reached in and cut the duct tape from my legs. Then I was yanked from the trunk.

"Take that sack off her," someone said. I felt hands reach down my side and pull the laundry sack up over my head and strip the duct tape from my mouth. It was dark, but not so dark that I couldn't see what I was facing.

Two men stood in front of me, another one off to the side moving behind. They weren't big guys. But there were three of them. I didn't think I had a chance to escape. I couldn't outrun them, not with my head pounding like a jackhammer. And, I had no idea where I was. We seemed to be standing in a dirt lot. If I ran, there was no cover to hide in that I could see. The fear that had been floating in the back of my head somewhere came rushing forward like a scream. I had just one hope. All three men wore black ski masks that covered their entire faces. If they were going to kill me, why the masks?

"What do you want?" I said. "Did Mark Miller send you?"

One of the guys took a step forward and slammed his fist into my face. I tried to pull aside from the punch, but still I could feel the impact smash the bones in my face. Blood started dripping from my nose.

"You see, now that's what you've gotta learn, girl," he said. "You've gotta learn to shut up."

He hit me again. This time in the stomach. My stomach cramped and I bent over only to be pulled upright again by the man who had moved behind me. My attacker kept hitting me in the stomach, the chest, until finally I was thrown on the ground. He kicked me until I lost consciousness.

The next thing I remember was hearing birds chirping.

It was early morning and light enough that I could see my surroundings. The car was gone. The handcuffs were gone. I was laying curled in a ball, in a dirt parking lot surrounded by dense stands of Ponderosa pines. It seemed to be a trailhead, though not one that saw much use. There was a single dirt road leading back through an open patch of meadow.

The drive down the dirt road had been short, so I knew a paved road, one with traffic I hoped, couldn't be far away.

Every move sent spasms through me. It was cold. Too cold. I must be up in the mountains, or at least in the foothills outside of Denver. Well, I could lay here and freeze or I could get up and start walking. Neither had any appeal. But walking would only hurt like hell. Freezing meant hypothermia, which meant death. Not much choice when you looked at it that way.

I pulled myself to my feet and bent over retching. That was okay. I hadn't eaten in so long that there wasn't much to get rid of. I pulled myself up and walked bent over like a pretzel. I cried with every step. As I walked I kept repeating in my brain, "I am so stupid ... stupid ... stupid."

When was I going to get this right? I'd seen it in Boston. Now it was staring me in the face in Denver. There really are people in the world who willingly hurt other people. There are people who play by different rules. Rules where the welfare of others isn't even an afterthought, where the only currency is power. This is something I'm going to have to learn if I intend to stay alive.

By the time I reached the road, the sun was well into the sky. Luckily, it was a Colorado state highway. There would be traffic along a road like this. I don't think I could have walked any further. I sat on the highway resting my back against a yield sign. It seemed like there should be some significance to that, but I passed out again before I could figure it out.

I came to when the EMTs were lifting me onto a gurney. An earnest young man was jabbering at a state trooper, waving his cell phone and pointing to the base of the yield sign and then back to me. I pointed my finger at the man. I wanted to know his name. I figured he must be my rescuer. I wanted to talk to him just so I could remember that there is at least one person willing to help a fellow human in trouble with no thought of gain. But the EMTs ignored me as they lifted the gurney into the back of the ambulance. I still didn't know where I was. But at that moment I just didn't care. I closed my eyes and let myself drift back into oblivion.

Chapter Twenty-Two

Bright lights overhead. As I rolled slowly under each one, it felt as if crystal shards were being stabbed through my forehead. I closed my eyes but still was assaulted by the cacophony of sound. There were voices nearby. One of them, I realized, was Linda. I thought I remembered at least part of the ambulance ride. How had she beaten the ambulance to the hospital, wherever the hospital was?

"You've got to be kidding," I heard her say. "She just got out of the emergency room. There is no way she is answering any questions now."

Gotten through emergency? I didn't remember any emergency room. I must be more out of it than I thought.

But, I wanted to answer questions. I didn't care if my head felt like it was split in half. I wanted to nail those guys that did this to me. I opened my eyes again, squinting at the light, and turned my head in the direction of Linda's voice. The world went into a tailspin, everything swinging wildly in a spinning circle. A wave of nausea swept over me, my battered stomach muscles spasming. All I could see clearly was Jessie walking slowly beside the gurney, staring at me, looking like a frightened little girl. I tried a small smile for her.

"Mom," Jessie called. "Mom, she's awake." She started shaking and broke into tears.

"Thank God," Linda whispered.

The gurney stopped moving. Linda grabbed my hand and leaned over me.

"Jo, you're at Lutheran Hospital. You've been beat up something fierce and you've got a serious concussion." I could hear the rage in her voice. "The doctors need to run a bunch more tests, but they think you'll be okay. You will be okay." She paused. "Listen Jo, it's important that you not talk to anybody about what happened last night unless I'm there. Do you understand? No one. I'm going to make sure there's always someone you know in the room with you."

"But the police," I whispered.

"Especially not the police, Jo. Or the FBI. Trust me on this. They just gave you pain meds. You'll sleep for a while. I'll be here when you wake up and we'll talk then."

Linda stepped back from the gurney and it started moving again.

When I did wake, I was lying in a bed in a hospital room. I could tell because of all the gizmos that were attached to me. It was dark outside and the hospital was quiet. A clock by my bed read near to midnight. So, it had been more than a day since I was grabbed. Linda was sitting in a chair, her head thrown back in sleep, her open computer tottering on the edge of her lap, inches from crashing to the floor.

The door was open and a policewoman was sitting in the hall across from it. Maybe she was waiting to talk with me, but it didn't look that way. More like she was guarding the door. That seemed excessive. How likely was it that those thugs would make a sneak attack in the hospital? Still I had to appreciate the thought.

I was feeling a thousand percent better, which wasn't saying much since I'd started at zero. Every part of my body ached and my head hurt enough to make me willing to trade it for a jack-o-lantern. I could tell drugs were still keeping the pain at a manageable level. But, I was thinking clearly again. Or, at least a whole lot more clearly than I had been, and that was what was important.

I could finger Mark. Maybe I couldn't link him directly to the guys who'd jumped me, but the coincidence was too much for the police to ignore. Once they started digging into his story, something was bound to show up. I just had to get Linda to lighten up so I could talk to them. And soon... time was wasting.

I didn't want to wake Linda. Clearly she'd had a rough day and it just didn't seem fair to rob her of what sleep she could get. But, I also wanted to get someone moving against Mark as soon as possible, before he found some way to cover his tracks.

Luckily, I was spared the decision. Linda's awakening was heralded by a crash as her computer hit the floor. She jumped up with a curse, grabbed it from the floor and looked at me.

"I'm sorry Jo."

"It's okay, I was awake already. I just didn't want to wake you. You okay?"

She put her computer aside and looked at me.

"We need to talk. Do you remember me telling you not to talk to anybody but me about what happened the other night?"

"I do, Linda, but I don't get why. I've got to tell the police what happened. It was Mark Miller. I went to talk with him to try to find out what happened to Latif. After I left him, these three guys jumped me. He must have sent them." I felt a twinge as I realized how Linda might react when I told her that they had jumped me in the driveway of her house. But she must know that. After all, my car was parked in her driveway.

"I'm sorry, Linda. I would never have gone home if I thought those guys were going to jump me there."

"What do you mean? You were abducted from our house?" Her eyes turned to knives.

"Well yes, after I parked the 4Runner in the driveway. I was getting some stuff from the back when they jumped me. I thought you'd realize that when you saw the car was there."

"The 4Runner wasn't in the driveway."

"Why not? Where was it?"

Linda looked out of the room at the policewoman sitting in the hall. She got up and closed the door.

I watched her. "What is going on, Linda? Why exactly is it that the police think I need a protective detail? What happened, and what does my car have to do with it?"

"It's not protection, Jo. You're under arrest. That's why you can't talk to the police."

I opened my mouth but I was too stunned to pull a thought out of my brain. Under arrest?

"What, did they find some evidence about the Messenger break-in?"

"It's not that. You need to take another day to rest. I'm bringing a stenographer in from my office tomorrow and we'll go over your whole story. Until then you need to gather your strength. You're going to need it. I'm seeing Judge Warner tomorrow afternoon to get a restraining order to stop the police or anyone else from questioning you until we can get a medical opinion about your fitness to give testimony. Even then we're going to want to be very careful about deciding what you can tell the police."

"But, I didn't do anything. What is it they think I did?" I didn't exactly scream. But I could hear the desperation in my voice.

"Jo, this is going to be hard for you. Are you sure you don't want to wait until tomorrow?"

Linda was about the farthest thing from a drama queen that I could imagine. If she said hard, it probably meant devastating. I needed to take her warning seriously. Still, how could I possibly get any rest with this hanging over my head?

"Tell me," I said.

Linda walked over and sat on the side of my bed. She took my hand in both of hers and held it there, gently stroking the back of my fingers.

"The state police were called in to check out the area after you were picked up on the highway. They found your 4Runner about 100 yards up the road from the trailhead parking lot."

"That's where they took me, to the parking lot, but they didn't take my car. They put me in the trunk of their car and drove me out there. My car was in the driveway at your house."

"I believe you," she said. She looked down at her hands, hesitant, and then up into my eyes. "They found Latif Brown there, too. Not far from the edge of the parking lot. He was dead, Jo, shot several times. The gun was not far from his body. Your finger prints were on the gun and they tested your hands for cordite. The results showed you'd fired a gun within hours of being found."

"No. No!" I found I was shouting. "No."

It was all I could say. It was all I could think. No, Latif was not dead. No, I had not shot him. No, I was not going to be blamed for this. I was so torn between grief, anger and outrage that I felt like my skin was going to split open. The Incredible Hulk would emerge and demolish the room, tear the building to shreds.

The policewoman was in the room in seconds, followed immediately by a nurse.

"I could never do that," I said. Linda squeezed my hand.

"Jo, stop talking. Now."

I did stop talking. For a moment everything froze.

Then I started sobbing. Sobs that grew until I was shaking.

Linda wrapped an arm around me, then looked at the policewoman.

"Thank you for your help, officer. Everything is fine here. I need to speak with my client alone."

The policewoman gave Linda a skeptical look, but turned and left. The nurse stayed.

"She needs to be resting," the nurse said. "I'm going to call the doctor and see if I can give her another sedative. But with a head and back injury like this, she needs to be laying still. Please try to keep her calm."

"Yes, I know," Linda said. "I will try."

With that assurance the nurse left. Linda leaned down and wrapped both arms around me.

"I am so sorry," she said. "There was just no easy way to tell you. I know you would never have hurt Latif. It's insane. We'll figure it out. It's going to be okay."

"Not for Latif it's not. God Linda, it's my fault. I'm the reason he went to Mark. And Mark had him killed. I know he did."

"You didn't make him confront Mark. That was his choice. He could have made a different one. You know what my Mom would say, you can't take responsibility for other people's choices. It robs them of the dignity they earn through the sacrifices they choose to make. Please try not to think about it now. I'll stay here with you as long as you need. Just please try to rest. You'll be better able to deal with everything when you heal."

I laid back against the bed and cried. At some point the nurse came in. I could feel the new sedative take effect and I drifted into sleep.

When I woke, Linda was gone. From there the day passed in snippets. As Linda promised, each time I woke a friend was sitting in the room. All I could remember was a few sentences of conversation with each person before I drifted off to sleep again.

Ed gave me an update on what was happening at the paper and in Utopia, which had at the last minute averted a nuclear holocaust. His wife, Anne, put in a shift. Other people from the paper came. Someone told me that Russ had practically begged for a shift. But Linda flatly refused, saying, "You don't board a fox in a chicken coop, and you don't put a crime reporter in a room with the hottest crime story in the city." That set me back a bit. The last thing I wanted was to be hounded by the press when I was released. The shoe didn't fit so well on the other foot.

I don't know how Linda worked it out with the hospital, but visiting hours or not, a steady stream of recruits sat guard by my bedside throughout the night until she returned the next day. The person I didn't see, one who I desperately wanted to see, was Hazel. Latif was her friend. She had introduced me to him. I needed to hear her say that she didn't blame me, even if I blamed myself.

Late afternoon Linda showed up with a young, thin, tall man. He was the stenographer. Somehow I'd been expecting someone different. He didn't say more than a sentence, just settled into a corner of the room with his little machine. Linda led me through recent events, beginning with my seeing Latif with Mark at the hotel, up through my waking in the hospital. The break-in at Messenger's wasn't mentioned, though she did question me about the information I had provided to Latif about Mark's ties to Messenger. She advised me to claim a confidential source as the provider of the information. When the interview was over the stenographer left and Linda stayed to talk for a while. There was no news about the murder or my status with the police other than that the restraining order had gone through. The police couldn't question me without a signed release from my doctor.

Soon Linda was replaced by Ben, which was a pleasant surprise. He was full of stories about his canine and feline clients and soon had me laughing despite my melancholy.

Still I must have dozed off. When I woke it was dark again. Hazel was sitting in the visitor chair wrapped in a quilt and reading. I just watched her. I didn't know what to say. If I hadn't walked into Latif's life, he'd still be alive, regardless of what Linda said about the choices he made. I couldn't help but feel responsible. But that's not what Hazel would want to hear. She'd lost too many good friends to good causes. People who had stood up to racism, misogyny, dictators, genocide. None of that would make the loss of Latif any easier, but my guilt wouldn't heal her pain either.

"Hazel, I am so sorry. Latif was a good man."

She looked up at me. Her eyes were sad but she smiled a faint smile.

"And you are a good woman, Jo. Don't blame yourself for this. You didn't deceive him, you didn't kill him. We will all work to see that justice is done here. In the meantime, my daughter tells me that I am here to guard you from the zealous officers of the law. I was looking forward to that, but so far no one has shown up. I expect my own zealous daughter has scared them all off."

"Do you know what's going on?" I looked out the door and saw the police were gone. "Am I still under arrest?"

"Your status is under discussion. I guess some of the evidence isn't holding up all that well. They're having a hard time explaining how you could have given a 230 pound man like Latif such a serious beating, for example. You may be fierce, but it doesn't seem likely to anyone that you could have taken him in a fight."

I remembered just the size of Latif's hands. I didn't think there were too many people in town who could have taken him one-on-one.

"So, I'm off the hook?"

"Not entirely. The FBI is floating the idea that you could have had an accomplice. They're still trying to nail you for the break-in at Messenger's. If you had an accomplice, it would make their job easier."

"Right, and after we killed Latif, this accomplice beat me up just to make my story look good. With accomplices like that they're not going to have to worry about my having a long criminal career."

"Yes, well that's essentially what Cap told them. Only he wasn't nearly so calm about it."

"I didn't realize that Cap was involved with this."

"Of course he is, Jo. We're all pulling for you."

"When can I leave here and go home?"

"In a couple of hours."

"Tonight?"

"Yes. Word on the street is that you're being released tomorrow morning. So we're taking you out of here tonight to avoid any hoopla. You'll be coming to stay with me for a while. It will be safer for everyone that way."

"Not for you."

She smiled. "I've always found safety to be much overrated."

Chapter Twenty-Three

It was midnight when a nurse showed up in my hospital room with a wheelchair. Hazel had stayed with me. As we left the room, no one was in sight. We whisked past the nurses' station.

The corridors were empty, quiet, the patients snug in their beds. The elevator took us down to the basement where we moved past deserted labs and the empty cafeteria. I wondered if the morgue was down here someplace. It seemed like the silent, abandoned place where a morgue would be hidden in a teenage horror flick.

Just when it was starting to feel like Halloween had arrived early, we exited through a small door to the underground parking lot. A narrow staircase led down to the pavement where Linda was waiting in her black SUV. Hazel helped me down the stairs while the nurse disappeared back into the hospital with the wheelchair. I struggled into the backseat of the car. I don't know if it was the ride through the hospital maze or just the lingering effects of the concussion, but my head was spinning. I'd been out of bed for 15 minutes and already all I wanted to do was lay back down. Hazel pulled herself into the seat beside me and Linda took off through the dark parking lot.

There was little traffic, but Linda crouched over the steering wheel, her head sweeping back and forth over the surrounding territory as if expecting an attack. She looked tired, and I realized what a strain this all must have been for her. Midnight was too late for her even on the weekend. I wondered how much sleep she was getting while I had lounged in the hospital bed. Sometimes it amazes me that Linda has stuck it out in our friendship. Linda likes order, predictability in her life. She's the kind of person who has all the books on her bookshelf arranged alphabetically by subject and author. But maybe that's the point. She chooses friends and lovers who cause the chaos and spontaneity that creates a kind of balance in her life, a balance she's been keeping since her mother and father started living separate lives. Well, that would put me firmly in Hazel's camp, and that was where I'd want to be. But I didn't want to cause Linda distress. It was good I was going to stay with Hazel. Linda would be challenged enough with the legal side of this mess. She didn't need to be acting caretaker at the same time.

The drive to Hazel's was a blur of flashing headlights and a growing headache. I nearly crawled from Linda's SUV to Hazel's spare bedroom, not even stopping to undress before I collapsed on the bed. Linda went home and Hazel went to make me a cup of chamomile tea to wash down the painkillers the doctor had prescribed.

Now what? I thought. I hadn't expected to be so weak or in so much pain. But sleep escaped me. Mostly I was thinking about revenge. At that moment I couldn't remember all the supposed stages of grief, but I was pretty sure anger was one of them. If so, I intended to take full advantage of it. I had a lot of revenge to plot. There was Latif's murder, my abduction, framing me for murder, and all the trouble and grief my family and friends had gone through. Then there was all the suffering Mark and his cronies had caused with their trafficking, the duplicity of Messenger and her sidekick Shaw. By the time Hazel arrived with the tea, I had mentally arranged for them all to live miserable lives of abject poverty and despair. What you sow, that shall you reap.

Hazel put the tea on the night stand, sat on the bed next to me and handed me a couple of white capsules.

"Do you want to talk about it?" she asked. "You look like you want to throttle somebody. That's understandable, but you're in no shape to get out of bed, much less go on the warpath. And you're in no mental state to decide on your best course of action."

Talk wasn't what I wanted. I didn't want to dilute my rage. I wanted to nurture it, feed it, make it grow.

"I appreciate the offer, Hazel. I'm just not ready to talk about this yet. I need time."

Hazel looked at me with a frown.

"Jo, I know you too well to buy that line. You do need time. But you would be the last person to recognize or act on that." She sighed. "Just promise me that you will wait until you are well enough to get around safely."

"I can't make any promises, Hazel. I just don't know what is going to happen next. There are too many people who need justice. I will do my best to stay safe. I promise that."

"Are you sure what you're talking about is justice and not revenge?"

"I can't see that there's any difference here, Hazel."

She rose from my bed and left the room without another word.

I knew I was causing her real grief. I could see it in her strained expression. But I couldn't help it. I was far past the turning point. Pain and this numbing fatigue were irrelevant too. I needed to take action.

The first thing I wanted to do was find Rosa. She had been so afraid when she had spoken with me. But Latif had reassured her, promised she could trust him to keep her safe.

Latif had been her guide off the street, her lifeline. What must she be thinking now? She must be terrified. It was my job now to keep her out of Mark's line of fire.

But first I had to find her.

I dragged myself from the bed with my head still spinning. I looked around. My purse wasn't in the room. That meant I didn't have my cell phone, and there was no land line phone in the room.

I could hear Hazel still moving around in the kitchen. If I went to use a phone in another room she would hear me and in all likelihood drag me back to bed. When I thought about it, of course, it didn't matter. Who was I going to call? I didn't know whether Rosa even had a telephone. But, when Latif was out of the room during my interview with her a few days earlier, Rosa had surreptitiously given me the address of the apartment where she was staying. In case I had news about Angela's murder, she said.

I lay back down and waited until I heard Hazel go off to bed. Then I waited again until enough time had passed for her to have fallen asleep. I slipped from the bedroom out to the living room. There was no light coming from beneath Hazel's door, and I could hear a soft snore. My purse lay on the couch. I picked it up and headed quietly out the front door. There were no keys in my purse. I suppose they hadn't found their way back to me from where they'd fallen in Linda's driveway when I was abducted. Of course I didn't have a car, so I didn't need the keys for that. But I did have a key to Hazel's house and I would have liked to have that with me. Maybe I could have gotten back into the house without Hazel ever having known I was gone. But there were no keys, and Hazel was going to be furious.

I pulled out my cell phone and called a local cab company. They were there in 20 minutes, enough time for me to question my sanity but not to change my mind. When the taxi arrived, I climbed in the back and directed the driver to take me to the warren of streets in downtown Denver known as Capitol Hill. Although I had the address of the building we were looking for, I had no clue what it would look like until we arrived. It turned out to be an old mansion remodeled into an eight-unit apartment. The driver parked the taxi and walked to the apartment entrance with me. He volunteered to stay until I needed a ride back home. He was a young guy, and either he was being gallant or I looked every bit as bad as I felt.

There was no elevator. Walking up the three flights of stairs to the apartment felt like a hike up Pikes Peak. My head was pounding worse and I knew I wasn't doing my concussion any favors. But that was beside the point. I wanted to talk with Rosa and I had no other way to reach her. It was close to 3:00 a.m., but I had no patience to wait for a better time or day.

I knocked on Rosa's door. Then I waited. I wondered how sound a sleeper she was. I hadn't expected her to be asleep. I don't know why. Sure she had been a prostitute. But now she had a regular 9 to 5 job. Even if it wasn't a work day, she would most likely still be in bed at this hour. I thought of turning around. But, I couldn't make myself leave. Maybe it was my own fear. I just had to know that she was safe. I had to know that the entire world wasn't sliding into a nightmare.

I knocked again and waited again. Finally I reached into my purse and pulled out my lock picks. Just your everyday American girl. No keys, but lock picks? No problem. I could only hope Rosa didn't keep a gun under her pillow for protection.

It took only a few minutes until I heard the lock click open. I stepped quickly into the room, pulling the door closed behind me.

"Rosa, it's Jo Walker. I just came to check up on you."

I quietly tiptoed into the apartment.

"Are you here?"

There was no response. I groped along the wall until I found a light switch and flicked it on. The apartment had been ransacked. Every piece of furniture was turned over and gutted. Books were ripped apart and strewn across the room. Shattered dishes were scattered across the floor.

I ran into the bedroom. No one was there. Rosa's purse was ripped apart, the contents thrown to the floor. There was blood streaked across the bedsheets. In that moment I knew she'd been taken. Maybe murdered or maybe put back in the brothel, but she was gone.

It started someplace deep in my chest. I felt it growing, building pressure, surging, about to break out. Then I started to cry. Part cry, part scream like a child's tantrum. I found I was smashing the wall with my balled up fist and I couldn't stop. It felt like I would never stop, like there was nothing in the world that could make me stop.

Eventually exhaustion won and I slid down the wall to the floor, sobbing. I heard voices and footsteps coming up the steps. The taxi driver, he must have heard me. Maybe he'd gotten help. Or maybe another tenant had heard me and called the police. But still I kept sobbing. This couldn't be happening again. First in Boston, then Latif, and now Rosa. How could I leave such a trail of death? And where was Rosa? I had to find her. I owed that to Latif. Dead or alive I had to find her.

Chapter Twenty-Four

I didn't get to take that ride back home with my friendly taxi driver. What I got instead was a ride to the downtown district police station in a patrol car. My banshee yells had woken several residents who had the police on speed dial. I was still huddled on the floor staring at Rosa's empty bed when they arrived. Within half an hour I was sitting at a table in an empty room at the police station, waiting for the cavalry. Only the cavalry didn't show up. A police detective showed up, but not Linda. I didn't want to think about what that meant. Linda always showed up. It was part of what being Linda meant. But for now it looked like I was on my own. And I wasn't in the mood.

I told the police what had happened, or most of it. I left out the part about breaking into the apartment. I claimed the door was already unlocked, which had alarmed me enough to proceed uninvited into the apartment. There hadn't been any breaking and entering, just a concerned friend. I doubt they believed me, especially after unearthing the lock picks from my handbag. But who was to call me a liar? No one had seen me enter the apartment. The taxi driver had stayed at the building entrance. The other tenants hadn't emerged until I started the racket inside the apartment. The rest of the story was straightforward. I arrived, saw the mess and freaked out. I figured I was all clear and ready for that ride home. But they didn't release me. They just left me sitting in the room, watching the wall clock second hand endlessly tick.

It was 4:30 in the morning and I was just getting ready to confess to plotting the assassination of Jimmy Hoffa when my FBI friends walked into the room. Great, I'd been left sitting here just waiting for these two? And I thought I'd been in a bad mood before these guys showed up.

I swear the FBI guy looked like he was smirking. It was his, "I've got you right where I want you now" look. The woman was as vanilla as ever. I figured my night had just gotten a whole lot more tedious. Might as well just get this over with.

"I've already told the police what happened tonight. I've got nothing to add to that report."

The guy took the lead. His partner probably couldn't have stopped him if she'd duct taped his mouth shut. He was smelling blood in the water. So was I, but in my fantasy, it was his blood. Each shark to your corner, and come out fighting.

"Yes, well we've gone over your report. It's not very convincing. You expect us to believe that you just happened to show up at the apartment of this Rosa Esposito, a woman known to the man that you are suspected of killing. Her apartment is ransacked, her blood at the scene, and it's just a coincidence? You had nothing to do with it? I would have thought a good reporter like you would be able to come up with a better lie. Now, why don't you tell us what really happened?"

Maybe I was the one who should duct tape his mouth, but I really didn't want to get that close.

"I never said I just happened to show up at her apartment. I went there specifically to check up on her. I was afraid that whoever murdered Latif might decide she was a threat also. Obviously I was right."

"Yeah, like I said, we read your report. Not very convincing."

"Well, you seem to think you already know what happened.

How about you tell me?"

"You say Latif Brown introduced you to this woman. What was their relationship?"

The way he said relationship made my stomach turn.

"If you're implying there was some kind of sexual relationship between them, you're wrong. He was her case worker. He helped her get off the street."

"Did he? She was a prostitute, right? What makes you so sure he got her off the street at all and not just into his bed?"

Just for a minute I considered picking up the table and throwing it at him. Sure it was nailed to the floor, but in the moment that didn't seem like much of an obstacle. Then it occurred to me that he would have loved it. He was pushing at me, seeing what would crack. Well, if I was going to crack it would be when I darn well pleased, not at his bidding. I sat back, closed my eyes and didn't respond at all. And so we sat.

I think he'd decided to wait me out. He was going to make me blink first. The thing is, he had no idea what my night had been like. Straight from a hospital bed to a crime scene to the police station. My body ached. My head was spinning. I was exhausted. My eyes were already closed. I was more likely to fall asleep than blurt out some true confession.

I don't know how long we sat there. He broke the silence first. I wasn't sure, but he may have indeed interrupted a cat nap.

"You know what I think?"

"God no, I don't think I'm capable of predicting what you might think."

"You, Brown, and Esposito were working together. They helped you break into Senator Messenger's office. Esposito was an illegal immigrant, so it's not hard to see why she might have a beef with Messenger. Brown too; a burnt-out social worker with a grudge. But after the break-in, you had a falling out. You killed them both. Or maybe she helped you kill Brown."

It would have been almost funny if his expression hadn't been so damn serious. They'd been looking awfully hard for a way to tie me to the break-in at Messenger's. For it to work, they needed an accomplice for me. Well, they'd found two. Such creativity deserved some response.

I turned to the other FBI agent.

"And you let this guy walk the streets? You usually don't run into this level of paranoid fantasy outside a mental hospital."

His clenched fist landed on the table with a crash.

And with impeccable timing, Linda walked into the room.

She didn't look at me. She waved a piece of paper in front of the FBI agents and said, "Maybe you remember this court order. It prohibits you from talking to my client."

The guy blustered. "This is a new case. That court order isn't relevant here."

"Oh please. Do you think I didn't hear that last absurd accusation? Nobody. Not the police, not you, speaks to my client until her doctor signs a consent. I've already talked to the police. She is not a suspect in tonight's break-in. There is no reason to hold her. We are leaving now."

She turned and walked from the room. I followed behind, not at all sure that I wasn't leaping into the fire from the frying pan.

We stepped out of the building. The sky was just lightening in the predawn. Linda turned on me.

"You think I have nothing better to do at 4:00 a.m. on a Sunday morning than drag you out of jail? I've spent the past three days by your bedside worried sick about you, keeping the feds, the police away from you, protecting you from the press, barely sleeping. And the first thing you do, before you're even half healed, is run off like some thick-headed action hero, throw yourself in harm's way. Do you know how scared I've been? Then to be woken in the middle of the night with a call from the police. This is how you repay me?"

She broke into tears and stormed to her SUV.

It was then that I remembered it had only been two years since Linda had lost her husband, killed in a car accident. Days in the hospital, a late night call from the police. The memories must be churning.

I climbed into the car beside her. "I'm sorry, Linda. I just . . . you know how I am, sometimes I don't think. I just have to know. I get stuck on a track. It's like an obsession. I'm sorry."

"Yeah, I know. It's not enough, but I know."

She started the car and headed south away from the police station.

"I spoke to my mother. I called her on the way to the station. I woke her. She didn't even know you were gone. She was furious. You can only hope she's calmed down before we get back to her place. Once she figured out you were safe, she wanted me to just leave you at the police station. Said it was the only way to teach you to stop acting like a two year old. I think she meant it, too. I was tempted."

Hazel had probably figured out what effect my actions would have had on Linda. I was surprised she was willing to let me come back to her house at all. Linda and Hazel may not agree on much of anything, but that doesn't stop Hazel from being fiercely protective of her daughter.

I sat quietly in the car, thinking. I was in a mess. Linda was scared. Hazel was furious. They would both forgive me. I knew that. The problem was that I didn't think I could do anything differently. Rosa was still missing, and now I knew she was in danger . . . if she was even still alive. Maybe the police were looking for her. But they wouldn't be willing to do what I was to find her. I was just being delivered from my first attempt to locate Rosa and I was already planning my next move. That move didn't include lying in bed for the next couple of days, even if it would be a comfort to the people who cared for me. What I'd said to Linda was true. It was like an obsession and I didn't think I could stop.

Hazel greeted me at the door with a tired look. Handing me several pills and a glass of water, she said, "Take these and go to bed, Jo. We can talk about this when we've both had some rest."

I took the pills, a couple for pain and one for the nausea from the head injury. Taking them reminded me of how recently I'd been in the hospital and what bad shape I was still in. As if my aching body wasn't enough of a reminder. But as I lay waiting for the pills to take effect, I wasn't thinking about healing. I was thinking about Rosa.

The next step seemed obvious. I just had to find a way to get out the door without Hazel tying me to the bed.

It might have been the smells that woke me. The last food I'd had was dinner at the hospital. It hadn't been bad for hospital food, but it had been hospital food. This smell was home cooking, and, I realized, it smelled a lot more like dinner than breakfast.

I got out of bed slowly, listening to muted voices from another room. I hurt, but at least my head wasn't spinning like a roulette table. It might hurt to move, but I was ready for action, more or less.

I walked out to see Hazel and Cap sitting at the dining room table. Their reaction told me one thing: I was overdue for a shower and some personal grooming. When I came back from that, squeaky clean and primped, they were still sitting at the table, but now there was another place setting.

I slid into the chair mesmerized by what was really a simple menu of baked chicken and sides. Hazel just nodded and I settled back to eat. Cap, it seemed, had been appointed spokesman.

"Jo, you are too old for me to lecture you about what happened last night. But, what were you thinking? You don't even know how to defend yourself in a fight. You've had proof enough of that in the last few days. What if the people who killed Latif had been at Rosa's last night? Do you think there is anything you could have done to protect her? Or yourself for that matter? You'd be back in the hospital, if you were lucky. What did you prove? All you had to do was call the police. They would have checked in on her and you'd know what you know now, without having endangered yourself."

I could have defended my actions. I could have ridiculed his assumption that the police would have told me anything about what they found at Rosa's. But I didn't. I was conserving my energy. I could see that the day was moving to late afternoon. I didn't have time for arguments.

"Cap, where is my car?"

He looked at me like I'd just asked him where to find the yellow brick road. He'd been expecting a fight; instead he'd gotten a total non sequitur. It took him a moment to recover.

"What? Why?"

"It's my only transportation. I need it."

"Why do you need transportation? You're supposed to be staying in bed for at least another day. If you need something, one of us can pick it up for you."

"I can't stay. I've got to go see Rivera."

Hazel stood up, sputtered and sat back down without saying a coherent word.

"Look," I said, "if Rosa is dead, there's nothing I can do about it. You're right. But if they've taken her back to a brothel, Rivera will know about it. At least, I hope he will. I haven't been able to pin down his role in all of this. But if he is smuggling the women in for the brothels, then he has some connection to Miller. Maybe he didn't have anything to do with Latif's murder, but at the least he'll be able to find out if Rosa landed back in a brothel, and if so, where

I can find her.

"Cap, you may not agree with my suspicions about Rivera. But what if I'm right about what has happened to Rosa? It won't take them long to make her disappear into a brothel in another state. We'll never find her then. She had the courage to get out, Cap. Isn't she worth the risk of being wrong? All I'm asking is your help in getting my car back."

I looked at Hazel.

"And your patience. It's not like Rivera is going to shoot me in his living room," I added.

"Your car is in the police impound lot. They are not going to give it back to you any time in the near future."

"So, I'll need to find other transportation. Maybe I can rent a car."

"I'll drive you," Cap said.

Hazel and I both looked at him stunned. He just shrugged his shoulders.

"It's like you said this morning, Hazel. It's like trying to change the course of a tornado. Maybe at least I can minimize some of the damage."

Chapter Twenty-Five

Cap was driving a Chevy pickup that was probably young about the same time he was. I knew for a fact that he owned a new sedan, but I'd never seen him drive it. At least the pickup was in good working order without screeching brakes or a billowing smoke trail. That's all I cared about, transportation that wouldn't announce our arrival to the household or scare the neighbors into calling the fire department.

I'd been to Rivera's house less than a week ago, though it sure seemed a lot longer, when I'd trailed Luis to the meeting with Shaw. Only this time we pulled into the large circular drive that fronted his house.

My knock brought a small, wiry woman to the door. She looked me up and down, taking in the bruises from my recent abduction that were just ripening to a deep bluish green. She turned to Cap.

"Yes, may I help you?"

I leaped in. "We're here to see Mr. Rivera. Is he home?"

"You have an appointment?"

"No, I didn't have time to make one. I thought we'd just drop by. I'm sure he'll see us."

I tried for an ingratiating smile, but the woman took a couple of steps backwards. So I'm thinking I probably need to work on ingratiating.

"He is busy. You make an appointment and come back."

"I'm sorry, but I really can't wait. I'm with the newspaper. If you'll just tell him he has visitors, we'll wait right here."

The poor woman was looking increasingly distressed. But she moved closer to block the doorway. Cap was shifting uneasily behind me.

"Listen Jo, it's Sunday afternoon. The guy is probably having dinner with his family. You can't just bully your way into his house."

Actually, that's exactly what I was planning to do. I'd known from the get go that bringing Cap wasn't the best idea. I wasn't expecting Rivera to roll out the red carpet for me. But it had been the only way to get past Hazel and out of the house. Well, Cap was about to see me in action, in my tough girl mode, and I didn't expect he was going to like it much.

I made the woman's weight at about 110 pounds if she'd just taken a shower fully clothed. She looked determined, but in the last few days I'd been kidnapped, beaten, arrested, and harassed by police, the FBI, and friends. She didn't know from determined.

I wedged my foot in the door to prevent it from slamming in my face, leaned over her and yelled into the room beyond.

"Yoo-hoo, Mr. Rivera, are you home?" I felt a bit like a demented southern belle trying to force her way into a party.

Cap turned three different shades of red—from pink to magenta in seconds, and began sputtering.

"Jo, you can't...."

"Yoo-hoo, Mr. Rivera."

"Jo, stop that."

I could hear shuffling of approaching shoes and decided I'd better be on the other side of the door before reinforcements arrived. If they were going to keep me out, I was going to make it harder than just slamming the door. I leaned hard against the door and shoved. The maid toppled backwards.

I heard a gasp from Cap behind me. And felt his hand on my arm. I definitely was going to have to send this woman flowers. She didn't deserve this grief, regardless of who she worked for.

I pushed the door fully open and walked into the foyer, shaking Cap's hand from my arm. I was just in time to meet Rivera's bodyguard running down a central staircase into the room. He still looked half Rottweiler to me. Gorgeous but mean. Him, I was not going to be able to push past.

"Hey, Jose, I just stopped by to see your boss. Before you ask, no, I don't have an appointment. But you know how reporters are, can't hold the presses."

Of course *The Review* wasn't going to press for another week and I didn't have a story in that issue anyhow. But it sounded like a good excuse to me. Just reminding people that they may be in the public eye can open a whole lot of doors.

Jose and the maid exchanged a few sentences in Spanish, which essentially amounted to, "Go ask the boss what to do with this crazy lady." Well maybe it wasn't lady, but my Spanish isn't good enough to cross into more colorful language.

She left the room and Jose planted himself like a giant redwood in the path to the rest of the house. Arms folded across his chest. It looked like he was begging me to cross him. And I thought about it. Tough guy power theatrics bring out the worst in me. I figured I could at least make faces at him like the tourists at Buckingham Palace who taunt the guards to see if they can make them twitch. If Cap hadn't been there, I might have. But Cap had already seen enough bad behavior from me today. I didn't want him to see me at my juvenile worst. The good news with Cap was that no matter what he reported back to Hazel, it wasn't like she hadn't done it all and worse. He wouldn't get much support for any outraged indignation there.

Speaking of which, I turned to see if he had followed me into the foyer. He hadn't. I looked him a question mark.

"There is no way I am going to enter this house until someone invites me in. And no, that doesn't include you."

I shrugged. I wasn't leaving until I saw Rivera or someone physically carried me out, so there wasn't much to discuss.

It was only a few moments before the man himself came striding down the staircase. I made Rivera to be in his early 60's, a patriarch in his prime standing in the heart of his domain. He was dressed in a navy suit. Who wears a suit to dinner at home on a Sunday afternoon? Either the mayor was a guest for dinner upstairs, or Rivera didn't believe in downtime. I'm sure he intended to look stern and offended at the disruption. But I was immune. I just didn't care about his injured pride.

Unfortunately, I also hadn't given much thought to what I was going to say. It seemed like a poor idea to start with an abduction accusation, but I couldn't muster any nice.

Behind me Cap stepped into the room, his cop persona taking voice.

"Mr. Rivera, we are sorry to interrupt your Sunday dinner. I hope you can spare us just a few minutes, to answer a couple of questions."

I hated that he sounded so calm, so apologetic. But I knew if I started talking we'd be back on the street in a second. I settled for skewering Rivera with a hostile glare.

Hazel was right, I needed to rest and heal, get some control back on my emotions. I was just too raw. Suddenly I was very glad Cap was there to carry the conversation.

Rivera meanwhile, was pretending I wasn't there. He looked at Cap.

"It's Captain Murray. Isn't it? I thought you had retired, Captain."

"Yes, I have. But a friend of mine was recently killed and I'm helping with the investigation."

I wondered if that was true. Was Cap actually working with the police? I hadn't thought so. But Latif had been his friend through Hazel, so maybe he was, unofficially. At any rate, Rivera didn't question him.

"I assume you mean Mr. Brown. He was a credit to his organization. I'm sure he'll be missed. But I don't see what information I could possibly have about his death."

"Well, a former client of his has also disappeared. A woman named Rosa Esposito. Perhaps you have heard of her through your ties to the Latino community."

Rivera turned and finally looked at me. He flinched momentarily at the sight of my bruised face, but chose not to comment. When he'd quickly recovered his composure, his own glare became more than a match for mine.

"I suppose what you mean is that this reporter has been telling tales about how I've been smuggling sex workers illegally into the country. How I'm running a string of brothels filled with young women I've stolen from their homes and forced into prostitution."

With all the wounded indignation of the falsely accused, he turned to Cap again.

"None of it is true. It is just a pack of lies she's concocted to discredit me, to tarnish my name, to shame my family. If this is your source, I'll have to ask you to leave, Captain. I'd be happy to help with your investigation in any way I can. And I will see if I can find any information to help you locate Miss Esposito. But if you want my help, don't approach me again in the company of this woman. Now please leave before I call the Police Commissioner to determine just how official your involvement in this matter is."

Rivera turned and walked back up the staircase, leaving Jose to guard the rear. I was ready to charge up the stairs after him. But this time Cap's restraining grip on my arm was a vise.

He watched Rivera's retreating back. "Well, now isn't that interesting. Come on Jo, we're not going to find out anything else here."

I followed Cap out to the truck, not sure what to make of his reaction. I had expected him to be embarrassed or angry with me for dragging him into such an uncomfortable situation. But on the drive back to Hazel's he just sat wordless until I broke the silence.

"Listen, Cap, I'm sorry. I didn't want to drag you into that situation. I just had to find out what he knew."

"And what did you find out?"

"Nothing really. I don't know what I expected. I guess I was just hoping for a blunder, that by surprising him maybe he would say something he didn't mean to. The visit didn't amount to much."

"Jo, I've interviewed a lot of suspects. Some who were guilty and some who were innocent. The one thing I can say for sure is that Rivera is not innocent. There is something he is hiding. I'm not saying he knows anything about Rosa or Latif. But that much bluster is covering something."

"But how do I find out what? I'm afraid I'm running out of time."

"Well, I can tell you the police are not going to go after Rivera, not without some real evidence, which I might remind you, you don't have. I would suggest you call your crime reporter friend at the *Post*. What was his name, Russ? Even if he doesn't know anything, he's likely to have the contacts to help you ferret out the information. I know you don't really trust the guy, but I had a couple of conversations with him while he was trying to get in to see you at the hospital. He might surprise you. He's got the kind of job that makes him see the worst in people. But he definitely thinks you are one of the good guys. I think he'd like to help."

The thought of an altruistic Russ put me over my limit. My emotions were just used up. I closed my eyes and didn't move again until we pulled up to Hazel's house.

Chapter Twenty-Six

I spent the next day at Hazel's trying to mend fences. I hadn't been forgiven for leaping out of my sick bed to run after Rivera. It felt mighty cold in that house for a spring day.

After lunch Cap showed up, waving a set of keys to his car.

"Here Jo, you can use this until the police release your car. I never drive it anyhow. I prefer my truck. Just don't use it in any felonies."

"Thanks, Cap. I appreciate it."

"And what made you decide this was a good idea?" Hazel said, anger deepening her voice.

"Come on Hazel, she's a grown woman. What are you gonna do, lock her in the basement? If she's going to pursue this, she's going to. Neither one of us can stop her. She's amply demonstrated that. We might as well see that she has safe, reliable transportation. Or next thing she'll be hitchhiking down Colfax. I've gotta run. A friend is taking me back home and he's waiting outside."

"Smooth, Cap, drop and run," I said.

We both smiled at Hazel, who didn't smile back.

"Seriously, Jo, try to stay out of trouble. And if it finds you, call the police or me. No more flying solo. These men are killers and we'd like to keep you around for a while."

By late afternoon, Hazel had shown no inclination to thaw and I was sick of being treated like a delinquent. I decided to head home to finish my recuperation. If the FBI was still after me, they could find me as easily at Hazel's as they could at home, and I wanted my bed. Linda would likely still be at the office. With luck Jessie would be off at a friend's and I'd have the house to myself.

On the way I made a quick stop at the office to check email and talk with Ed. When I walked in Skye greeted me with smiles and a hug. Not a bad antidote to Hazel's black cloud.

"Sorry they wouldn't let me take a shift with you at the hospital. Guess my parents didn't want me butting heads with the police if it came to that. If you are looking for Mr. Turner, he isn't in."

If Ed wasn't in, there wasn't much point in hanging around.

"I appreciate the thought, Skye, but I was pretty messed up at the hospital. I'd rather you got the picture second hand. How about I treat you to a burger at my place? I'll fill you in on all the gory details. Just let me finish up a few things in my office and I'll be right with you."

We climbed into the car in the dwindling light of early evening. I was just putting the key in the ignition when Skye said, "Hey that's cool, who left you the stuffed dog? Someone who missed you at the hospital?"

I looked up. There, resting on the windshield, staring into my face was a stuffed, floppy-eared, spaniel with a big yellow bow. My mind froze. That dog didn't belong on my car. It belonged perched amid a group of mates in the middle of Jessie's bed, whenever she got around to making her bed. What was it doing on the hood of my car . . . well, Cap's car? My brain seemed to have just stopped working. This made no sense. Skye reached out and pulled the dog into the car.

"Hey there's a tag on it."

I grabbed it from him before he could open it. The note read: "How many people have to die before you learn to mind your own business?"

The car was halfway down the street before I realized I was driving. A rage shook me so deeply that I had stopped breathing, not sure I could ever start again. With it rose fear.

If they had hurt Jessie . . . I just couldn't finish the thought. I wouldn't let it be true.

I don't remember the drive home. Skye sat in the car beside me but stopped trying to get me to explain what was happening. All I could think of was the need to get home and find Jessie. One scenario after another played itself out in front of me. Jessie kidnapped, bound, stuffed in the trunk of a car, terrified, and not understanding. Jessie attacked, injured, left wounded, unable to call for help. What had her plans been for tonight? Was she with Jill? Had they both become victims? I was torn between rage and fear, my hands trembling on the steering wheel.

I switched my headlights off as I turned into the driveway and slid silently to a stop. I knew I had to think clearly. This could be a trap, meant to lure me recklessly into danger. Or, it could be nothing but a cruel note meant to scare me. I wouldn't know until I went inside, but I had to go slowly, not taking the chance of being caught unaware.

The house was dark; there was no light showing through the closed blinds. I opened the car door and paused. It was much too dark. I was startled as I realized the motion detector hadn't flashed on the lights when I pulled into the driveway. I tried to remember if they had been working the last time I'd been here after dark . . . when had that been? I was almost sure they had. I pulled back in the car and closed the door again quickly so I wouldn't be exposed by the interior light.

Skye was sitting motionless in the passenger seat. Having given up on getting any answers from me, he must have been creating his own explanations. Clearly they weren't pleasant. He looked confused and frightened.

I handed him the note.

"Skye, listen, this may not mean anything, but I need to go check this out and I want you to stay in the car." He started to protest, but I held up my hand and said, "Don't argue, just stay."

Quickly I got out of the car and closed the door silently behind me. With a pointed finger I signaled Skye to remain where he was and walked slowly around the house toward the back door.

In a way I was grateful for the dark. Though I couldn't see clearly, I knew I also couldn't be seen. And if there was an intruder, I had the advantage of knowing the house and the grounds better.

A rake Linda had abandoned earlier was still propped under the deck by the lilac bushes. I grabbed it as I headed up the back stairs. Not that I could picture defending myself with a rake, still it felt better to be holding something, and perhaps I could use it to fend off an attack.

It wasn't what I heard that made me pause again at the door. It was what I didn't hear. There were no voices, no sounds of the television or radio. Even if Linda and Jessie were out, I should have heard Bosco scratching at the door in anticipation of my arrival. The house was silent in a way that was not normal.

I reached out with my keys, but before I could unlock it, the door swung slowly inward. It had been jimmied open. I felt a scream growing in me. I wanted to race into the house yelling Jessie's name. But I forced myself to stop. I couldn't help Jessie if I was caught myself. I needed backup. If something happened to me, I couldn't leave Jessie unprotected. I stepped back until I could see the car. Even in the dark I could see that the interior was empty. Where was Skye? As I was composing all the parental admonitions I knew, I saw him silently coming toward me along the edge of the house.

As he crept up the back stairs I covered the damaged lock with my coat.

"Skye, I want you to go next door, get Bill. Tell him to call for help."

Skye just looked at me.

"If something's wrong I'm not going to just leave you," he said. His voice was tight but the look he gave me was determined.

"Skye, I know you want to help. The best help you can give me right now is to get the police. I don't even know if there's anything wrong. Just go, Skye, it's fine. I'll take care of Jessie." I pushed him gently. "Now, Skye. I need you to get help now."

He hesitated, took one more look at the door, crept back down the stairs and sprinted off toward Bill's house.

I couldn't wait for the help he was after. I pushed the door gently and stepped cautiously into the family room. There wasn't a sound in the house, not so much as the tinkling of the wind chimes from the deck. I couldn't imagine where Bosco was, unless Jessie had gone out and taken him along. There was a glimmer of hope in that thought. I closed the door behind me. The house was dimly lit by streetlights out front. I took a deep breath, trying to hold in my cascading fear. I stepped past the entrance to the living room and into the kitchen, feeling my way blindly around the kitchen table.

My foot brushed against a bundle on the floor. It gave gently against my step like a bundle of soft fabric. I reached down to move it out of my way and instead felt the soft yield of fur. It was Bosco. I tried to feel for breath, but his body was perfectly still. No sound, no breath, no movement. When I pulled my hand back it was wet and I knew with horror that it must be blood. His shoulder and flank were covered with blood.

"Oh my God, Bosco, what happened to you?" I knelt down and stroked him, but there was no response.

There was nothing I could do. Not now. I didn't know if the person who did this was still in the house.

"I need to find Jessie, Bosco. I'll be back," I mumbled, still stroking his head. "Good dog."

Pulling away from him, I set aside the rake and fumbled my hands across the kitchen counter until I found the knife block. I pulled the 8" carver from its slot. I wasn't thinking anymore of simply warding off an attack. Someone had broken into the house, and if they were still here, I was prepared to fight them. I turned toward the stairs to the bedrooms and froze. I knew I had heard a noise behind me, faint but not my imagination. Someone was still in the house. There it was again, a nearly silent shuffling noise, someone feeling their way through an unknown room. I stepped behind the counter and squatted out of sight, the knife held tightly in both hands pointed at the sound. It wasn't long before a tall dark shape moved stealthily across the doorway, a handgun held straight out in front of him. I held my position, waiting for the man to move past me into the room. I wasn't going to face that gun, an attack from behind was my only chance. I would have preferred a heavy weapon to knock him out, but the knife was what I had. I couldn't afford to give him a chance to fight back.

I did have another advantage, though. He didn't know the house as well as I did. Walking into the room, he bumped into the table, giving me a clear idea of where he was and the direction he was moving. Then I heard a soft thud as he stepped into Bosco. There was no sound for a moment and then a single word.

"Damn."

That one word brought me up short. It sounded surprised and upset, not the voice of the person responsible for the attack. Still I held my place. It couldn't be the police, not yet. Who else would be in the house? When the man walked past me, turning to head to the stairs, the answer became obvious. It was Bill. Not the Bill I knew, my neighbor who planted peonies and was helping Jessie rebuild her father's old car, but still Bill. In the mist of my anger and fear I wondered briefly what exactly he had done in the military. He moved like a professional, a handgun held arm's length in front, sliding cautiously through the room, intently focused. I called his name softly and he turned without a flinch, signaling me to get back down.

He walked to me in a crouch and placed his hand gently on my shoulder.

"You stay here," he whispered. He then turned, sharply sidestepping Bosco's body, and started up the stairs.

That was not going to happen. Bosco was lying on the floor, perhaps dead, certainly badly hurt. Jessie might be upstairs, hurt just as badly. I clenched my knife and started up the stairs behind Bill.

We went to Jessie's room first. There was no sign of her, but her room had been ransacked. In the dim light leaking through the windows, I could see clothes had been pulled from every drawer, her television smashed, papers and books torn and strewn across the floor.

Still moving as silently as possible in the near dark we went next to Linda's room, where the story was the same. The clock radio beside her bed was smashed, the sheets ripped from her bed. Someone had taken a knife and slashed all the pillows and cut pages from the books on her nightstand.

I was so tense my breath was coming in short gasps as we continued down the hall. We had just entered my bedroom when I heard the rumble of what sounded like a platoon of motorcycles pull into the driveway. It was the deep-throated rumble that only a Harley would make. When I sent Skye to ask Bill to get help, I had been thinking of the police. Obviously, Bill had a different idea of what kind of backup he wanted.

Within moments, two of Bill's friends were standing beside us with drawn guns. I recognized Daryl from Bill's picnic. He leaned close to Bill and whispered, "Ben and Ron are checking downstairs, but it doesn't look like anyone's here but us."

Bill nodded.

"We better light this place up and sweep the whole house." With that he flipped the switch to my bedroom light.

My room was untouched. Not a shoe or paper was out of place. Compared to all the chaos that I had seen in the other bedrooms, this was more disturbing. It was as if I were watching from the sidelines while those close to me were attacked. I walked further into the room and saw the envelope sitting propped on my pillow, my name neatly printed on the front. I reached to pick it up, but Bill stopped me with a firm hand on my arm.

"There might be finger prints."

He pulled a handkerchief from his pocket, lifted the envelope by the corner, and slipped a single sheet of paper from inside. Only two words were written on the paper: "Next time."

I started to shake from the inside, rage running through me like floodwaters. Bill reached to lead me to a chair, but I didn't move. I had thought I was angry before, but now I understood what a murderous rage was. If the man who had invaded my home had been standing in front of me, I would have pushed the carving knife into him without a thought. I was barely aware of Bill beside me, but I felt him prying the knife from my hand. I let it go. There was still Jessie to think of. Where was she? There was no blood upstairs. If anything had happened to Jessie, it didn't happen here. I turned and walked out of the room without a word, heading downstairs.

As I walked back to the kitchen I could see Ben, leaning over Bosco, rubbing the patch of bloodied fur between his ears.

"He's badly hurt, but he's still alive," he said. "I need to get him to the vet hospital quick. Bill, I need your car, can't take the pup on the bike."

I reached in my pocket and threw him the keys to Cap's car.

"Take this, it's in the driveway."

Ben scooped up Bosco and headed out the door. I couldn't see how badly Bosco was hurt, but I could see Ben's shirt where he held Bosco close against him. It was covered with blood.

Bill and his friends finished searching the house while I sat in the kitchen staring at the spot where Bosco had lain. I was still furious and could barely think clearly. But I had to. They had found no sign of Jessie. I needed to figure out how to locate her.

I was vaguely aware of Bill thanking the men who had helped with the search, and heard him call the police to report the break-in. Then he came and sat beside me.

"I told the police not to rush, that the house was secure. I thought we might need the time." He paused. "Skye showed me the note. Why is someone threatening you?"

"It's too long a story for right now, Bill. I need to find Jessie."

"Why? Was Jessie here tonight?" I saw a deep concern flash across his face. It spoke worlds about the bond that they were forming.

"I don't know . . . I don't know. But if she was here, then where is she now?"

I could see a fear to match mine take shape in his thoughts.

"Have you called Linda? Maybe she knows where Jessie is."

No, I hadn't called Linda. It never occurred to me.

How do you tell your best friend that you've endangered the life of her child?

I picked up the phone and dialed Linda's cell. She answered on the first ring. I didn't give her time to say hello.

"Linda, do you know where Jessie is?"

There was a brief, startled pause before she answered.

"Yes, she's staying at Jill's, some lame excuse about studying algebra, but more likely they'll spend the night on the phone to every teenager in the state." Her voice was light and amused.

"Are you sure?"

"Yes, I talked with her a little while ago. Why?"

"How long ago?"

Linda took a minute to answer.

"What is going on, Jo?" When I didn't respond, she said, "Just a few minutes ago. What is wrong, Jo?"

I started to cry, the relief washing through me. I thought of the risk I'd brought to the family. I thought of Bosco lying bloodied on the floor, the ransacked bedrooms. I wasn't ready to answer her questions. I didn't know how I ever could be.

"Just come home, Linda. I'll explain everything then," I said, and disconnected.

Chapter Twenty-Seven

I'd told Linda I would explain everything to her when she got home. But when it came to it, I couldn't face her. I left Bill to tell her what had happened.

I went to my bedroom. I pulled a suitcase from under my bed. I couldn't stay here. I was endangering Jessie and Linda. But was I leaving them unprotected? What could I do if I stayed? I was no bodyguard. Maybe it was Jessie and Linda who should leave. They could stay with Hazel until I could figure this out. But there wasn't much indication that I was going to be able to do that anytime soon. The answers eluded me. I couldn't expect them to leave their home indefinitely while I thrashed around.

I sat on my bed feeling lost and indecisive. As I sat there, Zephyr crawled out from under the dresser and jumped into my lap. I had looked for her briefly when I first got into my room, but hadn't found her. She must have decided it was safe to emerge. I knew there was little chance she would have been in danger.

There is a Native American myth. The Gods decided to separate man from the animals. A giant chasm grew between them. But at the last minute, just as the chasm could barely be breached, the dog leapt to the man's side and so has been man's companion ever since.

To look long into the eyes of a cat is to know that the cat never made that leap. The cat is still bound by instinct to nature's cycles of life and death. They know both the fear of the prey and the lust of the predator. They know that life is more often to the swift or cunning than to the brave. No cat would attack a prowler like Bosco had tonight. When attacked they hide, when cornered they fight. But it's the rare cat that volunteers for the battle.

Tonight I understood that battle in a way I never had before. Tonight I had been the prey. It wouldn't happen again.

I sat stroking Zephyr. I heard doors opening and closing downstairs. I could see the flashers of the police cars as they pulled to the curb. I knew they would want to talk with me, but no one came to my bedroom door. Linda's heels clicked across the hardwood floors as she went first to Jessie's room and then to her own. I heard first her exclamations of dismay, then I could hear Bill talking with her, softly urging her away from my bedroom.

"Give her and yourself time before you talk with her. She's not responsible for this."

"Well, if she's not responsible, then who is?" Linda's words cut into me.

"The men who broke in here are who's responsible, not Jo. Leave her be until you've settled down. You don't want to do something in your fear and anger that you'll regret later. Ben is taking care of Bosco and he's one of the best vets in Denver. If Bosco has a chance, Ben will see him through. Everyone else is safe. Appreciate that before you start throwing stones. You didn't see her standing with that knife ready to eviscerate anyone who had harmed Jessie. You don't see courage like that often. I know."

Their voices faded as they moved further down the hall.

When the knock came at the door, I thought it would be the police. But Hazel walked in. She looked exhausted. Her skin was nearly as gray as her hair. This was exactly what she and Cap had been warning me about, letting my zeal overcome my caution and putting people at risk. I had never imagined it would be Linda and

Jessie. I couldn't even look at her.

"Oh God, Hazel, I'm so sorry. I never wanted this to happen."

She sat on the bed beside me and rested a hand on my thigh.

"Of course you didn't. I can't talk about this tonight, Jo. I'm too tired and I can't think straight. We'll talk tomorrow. The police want to see you downstairs. I'm going to pack some things for you. You are going to come stay with me for a while. Where do you keep the cat carrier? We'll need to take Zephyr with us, too."

I nodded my head.

"But what about Linda? She can't stay here. She's the one who should go stay with you."

"Linda has already left. She didn't want Jessie to come home to this. She's picking up Jessie from Jill's and driving directly up to the cabin in Granby."

Linda's family had shared a cabin in Granby for generations. I hadn't thought of that.

"I don't know Hazel, that's awfully isolated. She shouldn't be alone. I don't suppose she wants me around, but maybe you could go with her."

"No need. Bill's following them up in his car. From what I've heard from him tonight, Linda wouldn't be safer with an armed platoon stationed up there. He seems to know how to take care of himself and those around him."

That was an understatement. And whatever I normally think of gun-toting protectors, right now I was grateful for him.

"Skye insisted that he was going along to Granby too, but Linda put a stop to that idea. I think that boy is taking on Bill as a role model."

Oh, great. First Hazel and now Bill. A radical activist and Rambo. His parents are going to hate me.

"I need to get him home," I said. "I nearly forgot that I'm his ride."

"One of Bill's friends already loaded him on the back of a motorcycle and took him home."

I allowed a brief, wan smile at that.

"Lots of excitement for that boy."

"Go downstairs and talk with the police," Hazel said after a pause. "Let's get this over with and get out of here. This place is breaking my heart."

The police were waiting for me. With all I'd been through with them the last couple of weeks, they weren't inclined to cut me any slack. I was frightened and I was honestly trying to cooperate. They didn't seem to believe anything I said. Or at least they didn't believe I was telling them everything I knew. Questions flew at me rapid fire, faster than I could begin to answer them in my fatigue. Repetitious and unrelenting. I might have spent the rest of the night standing in the kitchen, answering and re-answering their questions. Then, somewhere in the middle of my third rendition of events, Cap showed up. Within 20 minutes Hazel, Zephyr, and I were scrunched in the cab of Cap's truck, en route to Hazel's house.

No one spoke as we drove through downtown Denver. Cap had his arm draped over Hazel, who sat straddling the gear shift. Her head rested on his shoulder and I could hear her softly crying. Hazel didn't cry. In the years I'd known her, I'd seen her cry maybe three times. I'd never thought much about it.

Hazel saw so much suffering and so much injustice in the work she did. But that never made her cry. It made her angry, determined. She was crying now because she was afraid . . . afraid for her child, her granddaughter, maybe even for me. I felt as if I had betrayed her. I had to end this. I had to expose Rivera, stop Mark, and find Rosa, if she was still alive. I had to set this right.

When we arrived at Hazel's I locked Zephyr in the guest room and sat in the living room waiting for Hazel and Cap. In a few minutes Cap showed up with a pot of tea.

"Hazel's gone to bed. She's tired and just needs some time to herself."

I nodded but didn't respond.

"Don't take it personally, Jo. She's had a bad scare and she's angry. But she doesn't blame you."

"Well, I do. You both warned me that I was out of my league. And now look what's happened. I don't know what to do, Cap. I dragged Rosa into this, now Linda and Jessie are in danger. I can't abandon Rosa, but I can't take the chance of Linda or Jessie getting hurt either. I need to resolve this, but I don't know how. Do you think Rosa is still alive?"

Cap shifted in his chair and finally rose and walked over to stare out the back window. Following his stare I could see Hazel sitting on the back deck, dimly lit by street lights. She hadn't gone to bed, or it had been an unwelcoming place.

Cap turned to look at me.

"You're putting me in a bad position. I don't want you to keep risking your life. But, yes, I think there is a good chance that Rosa is still alive. These guys don't make money by killing off their merchandise. They'll probably keep her alive, move her to another state, and put her someplace where they can keep her isolated and intimidated but still make money off her.

"As for Linda and Jessie, they're safe for now. I think Bill would throw himself in front of a truck to protect Jessie. And Linda is no shrinking violet.

"But I don't have any more idea of how to end this than you do, Jo. I'll ask around the department tomorrow to see if there are any new leads. But I think I would have already heard. Why don't we sleep and see what new ideas tomorrow brings?"

"Aren't you going to tell me to leave it to the police?"

"I'd like to, but no. Seems like you may be the only catalyst that makes this investigation move. I don't like it, but I can't deny the obvious. Just don't play lone wolf. These guys are better hunters than you are."

Chapter Twenty-Eight

I woke early and stayed in bed late. Fatigue or maybe the desire to avoid Hazel kept me in bed until I heard Cap and Hazel leave. Hazel first, the quiet hum of her Civic, followed shortly by the louder roar of Cap's truck. I found a note from Cap on the dining room table. He reiterated his promise to see what news he could find at police headquarters, and to call me with the results. At the bottom, his closing statement read, "Stay out of trouble, or if you can't do that, don't act alone."

I thought about our conversation yesterday. Linda and Jessie were in hiding. Hazel was probably at the house now, cleaning up the mess left by the break-in. A break-in I'd caused.

I'd told Cap I didn't know what to do next, and he'd told me not to act alone, a warning he'd repeated this morning. Well, that just wasn't very helpful. I couldn't sit at Hazel's house waiting for him to dig up some clues at the police station. I was way beyond being able to just sit. I had to take some action.

I picked up the phone. I thought of Cap's suggestion that I call Russ. He was the one person I could think of who might be helpful and willing. He must be salivating for this story. Immigration, prostitution, political intrigue, even murder. It was enough to make any reporter drool.

I reached him at his office.

"Hey, Girl Wonder, I thought you were avoiding me. When I

tried to get in to see you at the hospital, I thought Linda was going to haul me off to court. I heard about the break-in last night. Everything okay?"

"Not really so much. Linda's dog got badly hurt, and it's too early to know if he'll recover. My relationship with Linda is, well, let's just say if you wanted to assault me now, she'd hold the door open for you and probably provide the bludgeon."

"Where're you staying? I'll be right over."

"I didn't call to arrange an interview, Russ. I need your help. I'll give you the crime angle on the story in return."

"Hey, Jo, I may be a bad-ass reporter, but I can tell you're in trouble. You don't need to trade for my help. Though, if the story happens to fall my way, I won't complain. What do you need?"

"That's the problem, I don't know. I know the players, I think I even know the game . . . well, most of it. I just don't have any proof, not proof that I can take to the police."

"So, tell me."

"I'm staying at Hazel's. Can you come here? I'm not doing this over the phone."

"I'll be there in 20 minutes."

He made it in 15. By the time he walked in the door, I was starting to form a plan. I told him everything. Maybe not the best competitive strategy, but I wasn't looking for a Pulitzer. I wanted this settled. I wanted justice for Latif, Rosa, and Angela. I wanted my life back. And yes, I wanted revenge. Mark had played me for a fool, he'd threatened my family, framed me for murder. I wanted payback.

When I had finished telling my story, Russ was looking at me like I'd lost my mind. But he couldn't hide the glimmer of lust in his eyes.

"Let me get this straight. You think U.S. Congresswoman Dorothea Messenger, the rising conservative, family-values icon, is taking secret campaign contributions from the manager of one of the most prestigious hotels in downtown Denver, who as a sideline is running a regional prostitution ring, and by the way may also be a murderer. And the ring is provided with prostitutes by Carlos Rivera, one of the leading Latino politicians in Denver. Is that it? Don't you think you can find a way to drag the governor or maybe a U.S. senator into the mix?"

"I know it sounds incredible. But I'm not crazy, Russ. I found proof of Mark Miller's campaign contributions to Messenger at her office. And I've seen the prostitutes at his hotel. I know he had Latif killed. He practically admitted it when he said he'd do the same to me. I don't know that Messenger is involved. But I saw one of Rivera's men meet with her aide Shaw at her offices."

"But you don't know what they were meeting about. It might not have had anything to do with prostitution. Rivera and Messenger are both politicians. Who knows what they might have to discuss?"

"Oh, come on Russ. Messenger and Rivera? What could they possibly have to talk about except how much they hate each other? Besides, these guys were meeting in secret in the middle of the night."

"Right, that would be the night before you didn't break into Messenger's office. Okay, it looks suspicious, but it's all speculation. I don't see what you can do with any of it. And I don't buy Rivera's involvement. I know the man can be a windbag, but he wouldn't turn any of his people over to a gringo to use that way. It's just not in his makeup. I admit he might be smuggling people into the U.S., but not for that."

"Okay, maybe it's someone else in his organization. Someone with fewer scruples about ethnic loyalty. Luis, the guy I saw meeting with Shaw, certainly could fill that role, and I do know for a fact that he's involved because of something that Rosa told me."

"I think you should talk with Rivera again," Russ said. "I know he hasn't been cooperative, but if you tell him what evidence you have, he might decide to investigate for himself. If he's involved, you won't be telling him anything he doesn't already know. And if he isn't, he's going to want to know the truth. A breach of trust like that in his organization could bring some real heat down on him. Just let me make the initial contact. I doubt you'd get in the door on your own."

"I'll think about it. But also, I've been thinking, there are a few things that don't fit. Like why did they kill Latif, but not me? He must have known something I don't. Or at least they thought he did. And why was Rosa's apartment ransacked? If they wanted her, why not just grab her? Why tear her place apart? There's something missing. Some smoking gun that Latif or Rosa had, or at least knew about. We need to find that."

"Any ideas about where to look, or what you'd even be looking for?"

"Maybe, but it's kind of a long shot. When I met with Rosa, she told me about a cell phone that Angela had swiped from a man she'd been with, after taking some supposedly incriminating photos of him with the phone. Angela had some idea of trading the phone back to this guy in exchange for getting her out of the brothel. Sounds iffy, *and* risky, huh? Anyway, Rosa advised Angela to go to Latif with the phone, and see if he could help her with that. Unfortunately, the phone and the pictures never made it to him. At least that's what Latif claimed. But what if it really does exist, and these guys are trying to find it?"

Russ looked skeptical.

"Whatever's in those pictures would have to be pretty bad for them to go to all this trouble over getting them back," he said.

"Or, *whoever* is in those pictures," I added.

He nodded.

"I see what you mean. But on the other hand, if the bad guys haven't found this phone after all they've gone through looking for it, what makes you think you can? Do you know something you're not telling me?"

I shook my head.

"I don't know anything at all, when you come right down to it. But maybe I can come up with a couple of ideas of where we might start looking. Anyway, it's the only lead I've got."

"Well, I think you have a better chance with Carlos Rivera. Let me call and see if I can get us an appointment. Then we can go and chase phantoms if you want."

Russ must have pulled out all his charm and clout because in a few minutes he was back in the living room with a confirmed appointment.

"Rivera will meet with us tomorrow morning at his office. He's booked up the rest of today, and he's not at all willing to have you anywhere near his house. I don't know what that's all about, but the mere suggestion of a meeting there tonight set him threatening to cancel the whole thing."

"Let's just say I haven't always respected his property rights," I said with a sheepish grin. "So, you've had your way, now I get mine. I want to go to Latif's house."

"Thanks, but no thanks. You're starting to make breaking and entering a career choice. I'd rather stay out of jail."

"Not a problem. I have a key to the house. Or, Hazel does, and I kind of borrowed it. Who's to say we're not just being good friends checking in on the house?"

"Probably any police officer who stops by."

"No guts, no glory, Russ. I'm going. You can come along or watch your big story ride off into the sunset."

It wasn't easy going back to Latif's house. We took the same route to the back of the house that Hazel and I had taken when we first discovered that Latif was missing. There were no dogs barking a welcome. They'd gone to live with Latif's sister. The house felt emptier than ever. When we got to the back door I reached out with the key, but the door swung inward without resistance. It had been pried open. If I had been alone, I think I would have turned and run. Entering another house that had likely been burglarized only a day after the break-in at Linda's took more courage than I could muster. But Russ pushed past me, his own survival instinct showing an uncharacteristic lapse.

Within moments he found a switch, and light filled the living room. Like Rosa's apartment, the place was trashed. Books pulled from bookcases, pages ripped out. Cushions slashed.

Latif's bedroom was in the same state. I headed into Latif's home office. There was a space for a laptop computer on his desk, but now the space was empty, strewn cables marking where the computer had been connected. I called Russ over.

"This is interesting," I said. "They smashed everything else, but took his computer."

"So what that means is, up to this point they still haven't found what they're looking for. They probably didn't have time to try to get around Latif's password into the computer, so they just took it with them to look at later. But keep in mind, this doesn't prove he actually had anything they wanted on that computer. It just means that the bad guys don't know that either, and don't want to leave any possibilities hanging out there."

I nodded.

"We need to go to Latif's office," I blurted on sudden inspiration. "Breaking into a suburban home is one thing, but a government office is one place these guys can't get into to search."

"Right," Russ said, "and we can?"

"If we get there before five, I think I can find a helper."

Russ hesitated, and I could almost see the gears turning inside his head. Until now he'd been skeptical and lethargic. Now he was on the scent. He was finally beginning to accept what I had instinctually felt all along. He nodded, then raced out to his car, pulling away from the curb almost before I could jump in, and drove through the Aurora suburbs with the pedal to the metal and his nose smashed to the steering wheel. We arrived panting in front of Latif's office door with 15 minutes to spare.

Marianne Boxer was easy to locate. Like many working at the anti-trafficking task force office, her days started early and often ran late. I greeted her and introduced Russ.

"Marianne, we're looking for some information that we think might help discover who killed Latif. I'm hoping you'll be willing to help us, though you may have to bend a rule or two to do it."

Marianne's smile faded to a reserved silence.

"The thing is, we'd like to have a look around Latif's office."

"Jo, that's not bending a rule," Marianne said. "It's breaking a whole list of them. What is it you're looking for?"

I'd been hoping she wouldn't ask that, because I didn't really know what I was looking for. Just following a hunch that maybe there was something....

"We won't know until we find it." It was the best, or at least the most truthful, answer I could come up with. I accompanied it with a pathetic, pleading puppy-dog expression.

She let me off the hook by saying, "Not that I wouldn't be willing to break the law if I thought it would help get the people who killed Latif."

She scrutinized us carefully before adding, "But I can't do anything that would break client confidentiality. You're both newspaper reporters, of all things. Latif would turn over in his grave if I let you go through his client records."

I couldn't argue that. I would never have even dared to make a request like this to Latif.

"We may not need to see client records. And if we do see anything confidential, we promise not to use any of it in any story we write. We won't write anything down. Mostly we are just looking for some photos on a cell phone that were supposedly sent to Latif, but that he said he never received."

I could see that Marianne was wavering.

"Jo, I think I can trust you. And, I trust *The Review*. But I don't know your friend. No offense," she said to Russ, then turned back to me. "I'll let you take a look at his office as long as I'm with you, but your friend will have to wait here."

Russ started to protest, but Marianne interrupted. "Those are my terms, take them or leave them."

Russ took them, but with small grace.

"I'm trusting you, Walker. You find something in there, you let me know."

I left him with a pat on the back, which didn't seem to reassure him.

Marianne went to a desk in a common area, which I assumed must belong to the administrative assistant. She lifted a set of keys from a hook tucked beneath the lap drawer. We headed to Latif's office, followed by malevolent stares from Russ.

Latif's office hadn't changed much since I'd last been there. I was surrounded again by walls covered with pictures of his clients. Some looking lost and hurt, some at play. How must these people feel, bereft of their champion?

Marianne was standing in the middle of the room looking around herself, as if she felt a bit lost.

"I still don't know what you're looking for," she said. "I can get you into his computer, but I don't have the password for his email account."

But I had already spotted the one thing in this office that most interested me, the one change from when I'd been here previously, and it wasn't in his computer. A tall stack of unopened mail was piled on the extra chair across from Latif's desk. A small brown package rested on top of the pile like a paperweight.

"What's that?" I asked, almost breathless.

Marianne's eyes followed my gaze.

"Mail that's arrived for Latif since his . . . passing. I've just been stacking it in here until someone with more authority than I have tells me what to do with it."

I stepped over and picked up the small package. It was addressed in careful handwriting to Latif Brown at the state office building address, but with no clue as to who had sent it.

"But what's *this*?" I asked again.

"The mailman brought that yesterday," Marianne said, with a smile that was somehow almost a frown. "Apparently it was dropped in a mailbox not far from here, with no postage and also no return address, so the post office didn't know what to do with it. I guess there's a fairly consistent pile of undeliverable mail that collects at the post office, and that's where this package ended up. But eventually our regular postman noticed it, and decided to just bring it over with the other mail. It was either that, or have it destroyed, he said. He told me it had probably been sitting there for a week or two before he saw it. If it hadn't been dropped at a mailbox in the same zip code, it never would have made it here."

"Any idea who it's from, or what's inside?"

"No clue," she said with a shake of her head.

"I need to open this," I said.

Marianne's expression was now definitely a frown.

"Tampering with the U.S. Mail is a federal crime, Jo."

"But there's no postage on it, so it's not technically U.S. Mail."

She brightened, and laughed nervously.

"That's right! Go ahead and open it, then."

I fumbled with the tape that held the box together, and when I finally got it open, a cellular phone spilled out. Without waiting for Marianne's permission, I pressed the button that would power it on, and when it had finished booting up I went immediately to the photo gallery. With Marianne looking over my shoulder I opened the first picture, and there was my answer.

It was a selfie. Sprawled on a bed, asleep, arms draped over the young woman who took the picture, was Jacob Shaw. So, that was the answer. Jacob Shaw, the pure and self-righteous Jacob Shaw, in the arms of an under-aged prostitute. Angela was dead because she had tried to use these pictures to get her freedom. I doubted she understood the hornet's nest she had kicked. She must have known Shaw was someone important, someone with enough clout to push for her release. What she hadn't known was that Shaw worked for the family-values queen of Colorado. And she probably also hadn't known that Shaw was secretly taking bribes for the Messenger campaign from the very people who were keeping her enslaved.

These pictures, combined with the campaign contributions, could bring Messenger down; destroy her political future and Shaw's along with it.

As I scrolled through the pictures, it only got worse. In several of them Shaw was fully awake, almost mugging for the camera, while engaged in a series of acts with Angela and another woman that I wouldn't have thought possible outside of a circus.

"Disgusting," Marianne said.

"You have no idea," I said. "I need to take this phone with me, Marianne."

"There is no way these pictures are going to the newspapers. What's the point? One more girl being raped by some lecher."

So I told Marianne the whole story. By the time I was done, her disgust had turned to fury.

"Marianne, you can't tell anyone about this. Not now. Give me a couple of days. It could put you in danger. And if the truth comes out now, we may never find Rosa. They'll make her disappear one way or the other."

Marianne plopped down in Latif's chair, looking exhausted by all this, shaking her head.

"I wouldn't know who to tell. It seems like these people have infiltrated every place."

I assumed she was referring to the task force meetings with Mark, planning the end of forced prostitution along with all of them. Betrayal, deception . . . no wonder she looked so shaken.

"We'll get him, Marianne. We'll break this whole thing wide open. I just need to get Rosa to a safe place first."

I headed out the door with the phone in my hand. I hated leaving Marianne alone, but time was short.

Russ was pacing in the outer office.

"Did you find anything?"

I handed him the phone, on which the photo gallery was still open, and watched his eyebrows shoot up at what he saw.

"Holy . . . this is dynamite."

"I know. But remember our agreement. You get the story after I get Rosa."

"And how are you going to do that? I can't sit on this story for long, Jo. I just can't do it. My innards will shrivel."

"Then let's hope your friend Carlos Rivera can give us a lead."

Chapter Twenty-Nine

Russ brought me back to Hazel's. Cap was grilling chicken for dinner. He invited Russ to stay for the meal. They settled in on the deck with a couple of beers. I found Hazel in the kitchen.

"Any word from Linda?"

"They made it safely up to Granby. I guess Bill made her wait in the car with Jessie while he made a room-by-room search of the house."

"Oh, I bet that went over well."

"Not so much, as you can imagine," Hazel smiled. "The last thing Linda ever wants to feel is helpless, especially where Jessie's concerned. And of course Bill wants to protect them both. If Bill and Linda ever settle down enough to have a relationship, they'll spend half their time proving who's tougher. But, I don't expect either one of them is thinking much about that right now."

"My money's on Linda. In my mind there's no muscle on Earth that's a match for Linda's *I'm-gonna-make-you-regret-that* stare."

"She gets that from her father. He could stare down a mountain lion. He also wasn't any better at accepting help than Linda is. Maybe I'm at fault there too. I wanted her to be self-reliant, a strong woman. Well, maybe Bill will figure it out if he decides it's worth the effort. I just hope she won't push him away. It comforts me to know that he's there with them."

"I don't think you need to worry about Bill. He's adopted Jessie as his own, regardless of what happens between him and Linda. You've seen them together. He'd protect Jessie with his life."

"Well, then heaven help anyone who crosses their path. They're both on high alert, Linda snarling at anything that comes near her brood. I spent the day at your house and got it pretty much cleaned up with some professional help. Though, of course, not everything can be salvaged."

"I'll pay to replace anything that needs replacing."

"Don't be ridiculous, Jo. That's what insurance is for. I want you to get over this guilt. It's not helping anyone. Save your effort for fixing the problem, not getting stuck in wasted emotions. Did you find out anything today that will settle this affair?"

The anger that had been missing in Hazel's voice now flared in her eyes.

"As a matter of fact, Russ and I did make some progress today. Why don't we join him and Cap on the deck? I'll tell you both about it."

Judging from the look Cap gave me when I walked onto the deck, Russ had already shared some of what we had learned.

"The chicken is done," he said. "Let's eat first and then we can talk."

"No," Hazel responded. "There is no way I am going to sit here idly talking through dinner without knowing what is going on. Either we talk while we eat, or we talk first."

We talked first, though our appetites didn't survive the discussion. Russ and I showed them the pictures on the phone, explaining as best we could about Jacob Shaw, and Angela's hope that he could rescue her, our supposition that she had died because of using the pictures to try to blackmail her way out of the brothel. And, how Latif had become a target when they (whoever "they" were) somehow found out that Angela had intended to pass the pictures along to him.

"This is a lot of damning information," Cap said. "But it still doesn't prove anything beyond the proverbial *shadow of a doubt*. You can place Shaw at the brothels. If your pictures are accepted as evidence, you can probably prove a connection between Shaw and the people operating the brothels. But you are a long way from proving murder or kidnapping."

"I hope when I find Rosa I'll have enough information to prove kidnapping. I need to find her, Cap. Even if I can't prove murder, at least I can get them in jail where they can't hurt anyone else."

We talked well into the evening through dinner, brainstorming ways to find Rosa. But we kept coming back to Rivera. Either he was involved and knew where Rosa was, or he could pressure Luis into revealing the information. If he was involved, all we could hope was to convince him to give up Rosa in exchange for avoiding blame for the murders of Latif and Angela. I was ready to give him a pass in exchange for Mark's head. Cap and Hazel were less convinced. Eventually Russ left for home and we all went to bed, hoping for a few hours of sleep before Russ and I confronted Rivera again.

When I met Russ the next morning at Rivera's office I was dressed in a black suit, black heels, and a starched white shirt.

Russ took one look at me and said, "Ah, I see we are going with the undertaker look this morning."

"If Rivera doesn't come up with something to help us find Rosa, it's his funeral."

Russ gave a deep sigh, his God, but you're a lot of work sigh.

"Why don't you let me do the talking? You sound like you're itching for a fight, and that won't get us anywhere."

I nodded. I wasn't exactly itching for a fight, more like prowling for a rumble. Best to zip it until I saw if Russ made any progress.

We were ushered into Rivera's office by his secretary.

Again Jose stood by the desk, his hostile good looks as usual a temptation and challenge rolled together. I wasn't in the mood to pay him any mind. Luis wasn't in the room.

"Thanks for agreeing to see us, Senator," Russ said, an unexpected reminder that Carlos Rivera had once served in the Colorado State Senate.

Rivera nodded a smile that barely touched his lips and left his eyes blank.

"I agreed to meet with you on the condition that this conversation is off the record. If you have something important to reveal to me about a member of my staff, as you indicated, then say it and be done. Though, considering the company you are keeping, I doubt I'll find any reason to give credence to your accusations."

"I think you'll find the information credible, considering the evidence we have."

"This conversation may be off the record," I added, "but that doesn't mean the investigation is off the record. We're here to provide you with information. What you do with it will decide how big a part you have in any press coverage that follows."

"Is that a threat?" Rivera bellowed.

Russ threw me a skewering look. "No, it's not a threat. Please, Senator, hear what I have to say. Maybe then you'll understand why Ms. Walker is so upset. There's no need for threats here." Russ glared at me. Then he softly addressed Rivera. "I know you'll want to do the right thing."

Rivera sat down behind his desk. "Well then, get on with it."

Russ began with the death of Angela and worked his way through all the events that resulted. He didn't conjecture, but he also didn't spare the details. He told about Luis' meeting with Shaw, Shaw's activities at the brothel, Mark's involvement with the prostitution ring. When he revealed the campaign contributions to Messenger from Mark, Rivera's eyes lit up. That was something he wanted to believe. Russ finished with the death of Latif and Rosa's disappearance.

"That's quite a story," Rivera said. "And my role in all of this is as Mark's partner, smuggling in prostitutes for this brothel ring with one of my men as the go-between delivering bribes to Messenger? You print a word of these lies and I'll have you in court."

"Before you call your attorney," Russ said, "you might want to look at these." He handed Rivera his own cell phone, to which we had copied all of the relevant pictures in case something happened to Shaw's phone. The first photos he showed Rivera were the ones I had taken of Luis meeting with Shaw. And then he showed him the photos of Shaw at the brothel.

There was a long silence.

"These could be doctored, counterfeit," Rivera said. But even he didn't sound convinced.

He had handed the phone to Jose and stared at his guard.

Rivera's look convinced me in a minute that for all his faults, he knew nothing about this. He looked like a confused child asking a parent to explain disturbing news.

"It's not possible," he muttered.

"They're not counterfeit," Russ assured him.

He looked first at Russ and then at me, as if expecting one of us to add something that could explain what he'd seen. I couldn't think of anything to say. It was the first time I'd felt sympathy for the man. But that didn't mean I wanted to comfort him.

He got up and walked over to look out the window.

"Leave now. I need to consider this."

"That's not good enough," I said. "There's a girl who's been kidnapped. She's in danger of being killed or hidden away in another brothel. There's no time for you to think about what to do. If you don't know what is going on here, then Luis does. You need to find out what he knows. Find out where they've taken Rosa."

He looked at Jose.

"We haven't been able to contact Luis for a couple of days. But I will find him," he added. "I most certainly will find him."

"And you'll let us know when you do? Look," I said, "I don't care about your political future. You want to run for governor some day? Fine. I'm not out to ruin you. But believe me, if Rosa dies or disappears because you didn't take action, I'll smear your name across the national press. And that *is* a threat."

"Your threats aren't necessary. Of course I won't let politics stand in the way of finding this girl. I'll have someone call you as soon as I find out anything. Now get out of my office."

When we had exited, Russ turned to me.

"You sure know how to kick a man when he's down. Obviously this whole thing was a total surprise to the guy."

"If it takes a kick to get him going, I'll come back with a soccer team. For now I need a gun."

"What? What do you need a gun for?"

"Everyone else in this game has one. If I'm going to mess with Mark and his crew again, I'm not going in without protection."

"Have you ever even shot a gun?"

"Yes! If you count shooting a 22 rifle at paper targets at summer camp. You own a gun, don't you?" It was just a guess, but there are a lot of gun-toting folk in Colorado.

"I do. I keep it locked in a safe at home and I have never shot it at a person, or any other living thing. But, I do take it to the range and practice. Which is my point. You have to learn how to use a gun and practice with it. You don't just pick one up and go chasing after the bad guys."

"Fine, we probably have a few hours before Rivera calls. Let's go to a range. You can show me."

"No way, Jo. In your state of mind, I wouldn't trust you with a water pistol."

"Then drop me at Hazel's. I'll call you when Rivera contacts me."

I picked up Cap's car at Hazel's. Mine was still in the police impound. I wasn't expecting to see it again until Hell cooled down a few degrees.

My next stop was the vet clinic. With Bill on guard duty in Granby, Ben was the only other person I could think of who might be willing to give me a crash course in firearms, acquisition, and operation.

"You want to borrow a gun?"

Ben sounded more confused than hostile. I took that as a good sign. Just being with Ben brought my blood pressure down 10 points. I'd shown up at his clinic and sneaked in to see him between patients. Ben assumed that I had come to check on Bosco. He took me to where Bosco lay hooked up to monitors and an IV. I stroked Bosco's head. He pushed back against my hand, still there, but not awake.

"He's doing well," Ben said. "Just groggy. I think he'll come through. It's still too early to tell."

Seeing Bosco trussed up like an ER patient was heartbreaking. I leaned down, kissed him, and whispered. "You did your best pup; I'm gonna finish the job."

That's when I told Ben again that I needed to borrow a gun.

Chapter Thirty

Rivera's call came around 3:30 as I was walking out of Ben's clinic. I was going to have to go *gunless* it appeared, since no one seemed to think I was firearm safe.

"We have a location for Luis."

"Where?"

"A ranch I own southeast of Denver. Jose will meet you outside my downtown office in one hour. He'll escort you."

"I'm not looking for an escort from your bodyguard. Just tell me where. I can find it on my own."

"Jose is going to pick up Luis at the ranch, and bring him back here so we can get this all straightened out. If you want to tag along, be outside my office in an hour. If you're not there, don't expect any additional help from me."

"Does Luis know that you're sending Jose to bring him back?"

There was a pause, then a terse, "No." With that, he hung up.

With hardly a minute to spare, I dashed back to Hazel's and changed from my go-to-meeting clothes into something more suited to bushwhacking through pastures and hay fields. I made a quick call to Russ with the meeting logistics.

When Russ and I arrived downtown, Jose was parked in a black SUV outside the office. Why do the bad guys always drive around in black SUVs? Maybe I should skip the gun and get a new car for that don't-mess-with-me image.

Russ and I both jumped for the front passenger seat. I beat him to it. With Russ pouting in the back seat, Jose headed west out of the city and south on I-25.

"How far is this ranch we're going to? And how do you know that Rosa and Luis are there?" I asked.

"Mr. Rivera sent out word he was looking for Luis. The man who runs the ranch for him called and said Luis was there with a girl that matches the description you gave. They've been staying in a guest cabin behind the barn, at the back of the property. No one knew they were there until the ranch manager went searching the place. The drive will take an hour or so. I'll let you know when we're close." His tone discouraged further questioning. And so time passed.

Russ wasn't happy with being shoved in the back seat away from the action. He kept jumping around like a puppy trying to whine his way into the front seat. I told him to just sit down, be a good boy, and stick his head out the window. But he was having none of it. He wanted to be part of the conversation, but of course there wasn't much conversation going on. Jose was sitting like a stone statue.

Russ lobbed questions at the front seat with the speed of a grand slam tennis match, but Jose didn't so much as flinch. When he got no response, Russ settled down on the back bench, pulled out his computer and started composing the story that I should have been writing. He was definitely going to scoop me on this one.

What was I doing? I was supposed to be a news reporter, not a vigilante off in search of a lost child. And what was I doing driving off to who knew where with a man who made the terminator look friendly?

I had called Cap and told him everything that had gone on. I wanted someone else to know we were driving into the heart of darkness, just in case Russ and I needed a rescue. I hung up before

Cap finished lecturing me. Who needed it?

Jose pulled off I-25 at Highway 86 and headed east towards Franktown. We were entering a rural area made up mostly of five to ten acre ranchettes, punctuated with a sprinkling of larger tracts of maybe 30 or 40 acres planted in hay or alfalfa, or at least something that looked to my city-bred self very much like hay and alfalfa should look. Gazing past the ubiquitous split rail fences, and along the unpaved lanes that led to the houses, some very small, some sprawling, but all set back a comfortable distance from the road, I began to form a clearer picture of what Rivera's *ranch* would look like.

After about half an hour we turned south and drove along gravel roads. Dusk was settling over the landscape. There was little to see but the dim outline of the scattered houses with large fields between. Probably a good location for a hideout from which to smuggle illegal aliens — easy access to the major north/south route from Mexico to Montana, few neighbors, just a smattering of cows, crops, and a whole lot of empty space. The hum of occasional wind turbines phased in and out.

Eventually Jose turned off the road onto one of the private lanes. A windbreak row of poplar trees lined the right side of the drive, with a shallow ditch running between the trees and the lane. Through the windshield I could see a modest ranch house ahead and to the left. Farther back, perhaps a quarter mile off, loomed a sizeable blue steel barn. Presumably the guest cabin that Jose had mentioned would be tucked behind this fairly massive structure. The lane, bordered by the row of poplars and the shallow ditch, ran the length of the property line to well beyond where the barn was located. Rivera's spread was evidently somewhat larger than most of the others out here.

Jose pulled to the left and came to a halt in front of the house, parking in a spot where the SUV could not be seen from the barn. A squat, middle-aged man stepped from the house and approached as Jose buzzed down the driver's side window. My weak Spanish couldn't follow the ensuing conversation, but from gestures I could tell the man was pointing down the lane toward the barn.

"Luis is at the guest cabin as we thought," Jose said by way of translation. "He's not alone."

"Who's with him?" I asked.

"The girl, and possibly three other men. The ranch manager thinks they may be waiting for someone else to arrive by plane."

"By plane?" I repeated, confused as to what that might mean. Then all at once it clicked in my brain. "You mean there's an airstrip on the property?"

Jose only nodded, then climbed from the driver's seat.

"I am walking from here," he said, "so that the approach of the car does not alert them. You can come if you want, but you must remain absolutely silent." Without another word he took off at a fast walk along the lane toward the barn.

Russ had abandoned his computer and climbed from the SUV to join me as I scrambled to catch up with the swift-moving Jose. I leaned close to Russ to whisper, "You did bring your gun, right?"

"What is it with you and guns, Walker? Yes, I brought it. But you can't have it."

"I don't want it. But that doesn't mean I won't take it if I have to. You've never been on the other side of this. I have. A woman died in Boston because I pushed too hard on the wrong people. I didn't understand the stakes. I was naive. I was playing for truth and justice; they were playing with life and death. That's not going to happen again. I won't be responsible for Rosa's death. If I have to use a gun to free her, I will."

An impatient sign from Jose reminded me that I had allowed my voice to rise to an unwise level. We were about halfway between the ranch house and the barn when Jose veered off the lane toward the right, crossing the ditch and putting the row of poplars between himself and the barn, and motioning for Russ and me to follow. Although by now the dark of night was nearly complete, I realized that Jose wanted whatever additional cover was available to help conceal our approach. It'd been quite a while since the trees had been trimmed of the shoots and small branches that sprouted near ground level. The leafy undergrowth afforded us a surprising degree of stealth, while at the same time allowing us to peer through the foliage to keep track of how close we were drawing to the barn. Even so, I heard the voices before the barn came clearly into view.

"Why do we have to wait for him?" That was Luis, but it was the second voice I heard that sent a chill up my spine.

"As soon as Shaw shows up you can leave, but not before." Mark Miller.

It was like a sudden blast of revelation . . . or was it redemption?

In one blinding moment all my crazy suspicions, suspicions that at times even I had only half believed, were confirmed. Mark Miller *was* the brains and the moving force behind the prostitution ring! For several moments I was lost in what felt like a shock-induced reverie, and when I came back to my senses, Mark was again talking.

"Because he caused this mess. And if the police ever question him, he'll give us all up to save his ass. I'm not going to let that happen."

Yellowish light spilled from a large sliding barn door that stood open. Luis and Miller stood just inside, oblivious to the fact that they were being watched and eavesdropped from about twenty feet away. I heard a soft click behind me and realized that Russ had pulled a small digital recorder from his jacket and begun recording the conversation.

Luis: "What else is there to do? I'll take the girl up to Montana. You told me you got a place ready for her there. I'll stay there until the heat dies down."

Miller: "I can't let it be known that I'm involved with the brothels. It will ruin the business in Denver, and the people I answer to don't accept failure."

There was real fear in Mark's voice, something I would never have expected. So, there was an even bigger organization behind him, one that wouldn't hesitate to hurt him.

"What are you going to do?" Now it was Luis who sounded frightened, or maybe just really confused. "Listen, killing that girl was Shaw's idea. I only did it because he told me to."

"Told you to and paid you well for it."

"Yeah, maybe, but she's dead and now this other one's gonna disappear."

"You're forgetting the pictures on that phone. Just because we couldn't find the damn thing doesn't mean that it won't be found."

"But the pictures don't show nothing about you."

"You think Shaw won't hand us all over? He'll finger you for the killing and me for the prostitution . . . try to set himself up as an innocent victim caught in a moment of weakness. Hell, he'll probably get away with community service.

"That damn reporter, Walker, isn't going to let this go either, regardless of what you do to threaten her. She's riled up enough people already that even if we kill her it will only bring more people on the hunt. We need a different solution."

I was relieved to hear that the target wasn't still on my back, though it was chilling to hear Mark talk about killing me as if I were a business liability.

"So, what's your different solution?" Luis asked, though by now I think we all knew what the solution was going to be.

"Shaw is going to have an accident and you are going to cause it."

"Why me?"

"Because you're the idiot who killed the girl in the first place. And because of you and Shaw I had to have Latif Brown killed. So, you'll take care of Shaw or I might have to take care of you both."

I could see Mark pacing inside the barn. He was losing patience, his voice rising in pitch. And I could now see that there were two other men with him besides Luis. I didn't know them, but I thought they were about the right size for the men who had kidnapped and beaten me.

Mark turned to one of them. "Where is that idiot Shaw?" he muttered.

I was thinking that maybe Shaw wasn't such an idiot and had decided to stay home for this meeting. Then I heard a car coming up the lane. I guess I'd given him too much credit.

A silver Mercedes pulled up to the barn. Shaw stepped from the car. So, maybe all the bad guys didn't drive SUVs. He walked up to Mark, his hand stuck in his pocket making a bulge that even from a distance I could tell was a gun.

Mark looked at it and said, "You're kidding, right? You think you're going to come here and threaten me?"

"It's just for protection. You call me out here and won't tell me why. What do you expect?"

Mark moved so quickly I didn't see the gun appear.

There was a shot fired and Shaw was on the ground.

"What I expect is to be rid of you and the mess you've made. That's what I expect," he said.

I couldn't tell if Shaw was dead, but he wasn't moving.

Mark turned to Luis.

"Get the girl."

Luis left at a trot, either because he didn't want to anger Mark, or maybe just to get out of range. Mark pulled the car keys from

Shaw's jacket and threw them to one of the other guys.

"Put him in the trunk, and get rid of him and the car where we talked about, where he can't be found. The last thing I need is for Messenger to start a crusade to find his killer. A disappearance will be harder for her to explain, especially when I leak information that he was taking bribes. Here, get rid of this gun too," he said, handing one of them his weapon. "I don't want it where it can be traced back to me."

Both guys went to move Shaw as Luis returned. He was pulling Rosa along beside him. Her hands were bound together at the wrists, and she was blindfolded. Her face was bruised and she stumbled as she walked. Seeing her walking beside him brought my blood to a boil. I felt Russ's hand on my arm. He was shaking his head and mouthing the word, "No."

I turned and looked for Jose. He had moved up closer to the building and was crouched in the shadows, watching Luis.

Mark walked up to Luis.

"You sure she doesn't know where that phone is?"

"If she knew, she would have told me. I made sure of that."

Mark turned and slapped Rosa hard across the face.

"Last chance, little girl. Tell me where that phone is and I'll see that you're taken care off. If you don't, well, you know how some Johns can be."

Rosa was sobbing. All she said was, "Angela said she would give it to Latif. That's all I know. I don't even know if she ever did give it to him . . . I don't know."

"That's not a very good answer."

To Luis he said, "The plane will be at the far end of the runway. Take her and get out of here. You find out what else she knows and call me. I want those pictures."

Luis grabbed Rosa's arm and started pulling her away. I had to do something. Russ tried to grab my arm but missed as I dashed from the trees towards the Mercedes. Shaw's gun had fallen from his pocket when the men moved him to the car. I grabbed it from the ground, turned and fired a single shot in the direction of Luis.

"Everyone freeze," I yelled.

Instead, everyone moved. The two guys jumped for cover and Mark turned, reaching into his pocket, only then remembering his gun was in the car with Shaw. Luis spun with Rosa in front of him and pointed his pistol at me. Before I could react there was a single gunshot. I watched as Luis' head exploded, spraying blood across Rosa's face. Jose stood beside me. His gun now pointed at the two men crouched behind the Mercedes. A signal from him and they stood with their hands in the air. I pointed my pistol at Miller. I thought about Latif and about Angela, about the women I had seen at the brothel. My hand started shaking. Evil was standing in front of me, and I could take it out of the world. Only I couldn't. But I so wanted to.

I felt Russ beside me, taking the gun out of my hand. When I turned and looked at him, I saw that he was nearly as shaken as I was. I let him take the pistol and watched as he and Jose bound the three men with ties Jose pulled from his jacket.

I went to Rosa and took her hand. It took me a few minutes to get the blindfold and straps that bound her wrists removed. I handed her a tissue and used another to dab the blood from her mouth. Then together we started walking down the road, away from the carnage and out into the cool evening air, not speaking, just walking.

Chapter Thirty-One

We were sitting together in Jose's car by the time the state police drove up. The ranch manager pointed to the barn. We didn't bother letting them know we were there. An ambulance followed soon after. I flagged it down.

There was nothing for them down the road. They soon whisked Rosa off in a cloud of flashing lights and sirens. I returned to the car and didn't move again until I saw Cap's old pickup pull into the road.

I spent hours that night and the next day with the state police, the local police, and the FBI. Cap stayed with me when they let him. Linda's firm sent an attorney, but I missed having her to defend me. I felt battered and hung out to dry. When they finally let me go, Cap took me back to Hazel's, where I collapsed in tears and sleep.

When I woke in the late afternoon, Russ was waiting with Hazel, Skye, and Cap in the living room. He looked like he hadn't slept since the night of the shooting. But he was smiling. He handed me a newspaper and I knew why. A picture of Jacob Shaw filled a quarter of the front page. The headline read, "Messenger Aide Implicated in Prostitute's Murder," and the drop head was, "Prominent Hotel Manager Also Involved."

"So, you got the story written?"

"Hey, we both did." I then saw my name in the byline beneath his.

"I don't think Ed is going to like this."

"I already talked with him. He wasn't thrilled with not getting the story, but you know *The Review* isn't a daily, and this story would never have held till the next issue. You got the byline, *The Review* got an honorable mention, and we'll all be living off this story for months, maybe years. Mark and his thugs are in jail. Messenger's organization is in chaos. She and Rivera are both hiding out, not saying a word to the press or anyone. Any dreams Messenger had for the presidency are gone. She'll be lucky if she can keep her congressional seat with all the heat that's gathering in her party and in the state. Rivera may be able to ride it out. There's no real proof linking him to smuggling people into the U.S., though it sounds like the state attorney general plans to dig around for some. Whatever happens with that, his political future isn't looking so great either."

"Geez, it's only been two days, not even that."

"The wheels of justice turn quickly when there's political hay to be made. Read the story. There's hardly a political leader in the state that hasn't jumped in to express their outrage. Even your old friend Duffet is trying to get as much distance from Messenger as he can. Not much loyalty when the ship hits the rocky seas."

I remembered Duffet following Messenger around the Immigration Reform Conference like an excited puppy.

"No, I guess not."

"Just don't answer your telephone. Every reporter in the state wants to talk with you, and a bunch of national news organizations as well. Mostly they're camped out in front of Linda's house figuring that's where you'll turn up. I didn't feel any need to provide them with your new address."

"Thanks, Russ. I've had enough questions."

"Well, I've still got some holes I'd like to fill in. Can I buy you dinner?"

Hazel interrupted. "No, you can't buy her dinner. I've got dinner in the oven. You're welcome to stay if Jo wants, but not for an interrogation."

"Sure, you can stay Russ. You had my back out there. Three questions and then we eat."

It turned into more than three questions. We spoke well into the night, Hazel and Cap with questions of their own. Skye sat in the corner of the living room, mostly silent, wearing an awestruck expression that implied he thought he might be in the presence of a roomful of minor gods, or at the very least royalty. When Hazel had finally pushed Russ and Skye out the door, she followed me into my room.

"Linda and Jessie are back from Granby. She called. She's worried for you. If you're ready, she'd like you to stop by tomorrow so you can talk."

Epilogue

I heard voices coming from the backyard when I pulled into the driveway behind Linda's car. I walked around to see Bill spraying Jessie with a water rifle while she squealed and ran for cover. Linda was sitting on the deck. Bosco was curled at her feet, his waist wrapped in white bandages. They both rose and walked to me as I climbed the steps to the deck.

"Bosco is looking much better. Is he going to be okay?"

"Yes. Ben brought him home last night. I think he was hoping to find you here. Ben said it will take time, but Bosco should recover completely."

"That's a relief."

"He also said something about you showing up at his clinic, looking for a gun. He was worried about you. I told him he could find you at my mother's house. You're planning to stay there for a while, aren't you?"

"For now. I'll be looking for a house to rent, but Hazel is putting me up until I can find something."

Linda reached and laid her hand on my arm.

"My mother called yesterday while you were sleeping and told me some of what happened at the ranch. That's why I came home. I had to see for myself that you were okay." She hesitated. "You understand why I can't have you living here, don't you? I don't blame you, Jo, I honestly don't. I did, and I'm sorry for that. It's just the way you are. You see an injustice and you just have to fix it, and once you start, you can't stop. I love that about you. You're more my mother's daughter than I am. But I was so scared, and I can't put Jessie at risk that anything like that could happen again. Jessie hates that you're not going to be living here anymore."

"It's okay, Linda. I couldn't live here after what happened. I'd always be afraid that I might put you in danger. I don't want to live with that fear. It's better if I get a place of my own. I'll talk to Jessie about it. It's not like I'm going to disappear from her life."

Linda nodded, leaned over and gave me a hug. "Thanks, Jo."

"I have just one request. Can you represent Rosa so she can get amnesty?"

"Oh, you haven't heard? That's already taken care of. I'm not an immigration attorney, so I can't do it. But Barbara Ezell in my firm is, and she's taken the case. The way Russ is crusading, Rosa is likely to become the poster child for immigration reform. That's right down Barb's alley. She'll relish the publicity and she'll do a great job too."

"Okay, another favor then," I smiled. "Do you have any more of that wine you were sipping on?"

"I'll go get you some. You might want to have a few glasses. My mother is expecting you to stay for the ceremony tonight."

"What ceremony?"

"The Shamanic Cleansing Ritual, of course."

"Hazel's idea?"

"Who else? Two local shamans and about 20 other people are coming over to burn sage, chant, and cleanse the house of the negative energy that was visited on it. Hazel arranged the whole thing. Jessie is excited. She invited Ben and Bill. And I think you owe it to me to be here for moral support."

"Yep, I think a glass of wine is in order."

"I'll bring the bottle."

About the Author

Karen Starkins was a journalist, technical writer, and manager who enjoyed meeting the challenges of writing and leading people. Her love of Colorado, both the environment and diverse cultural heritage, brought her to the University of Colorado and then later to the Denver area where she lived most of her adult life. She was a champion of Women's Rights, Human Trafficking, the environment, and her beloved cats. (at age of 72)

When Karen died in 2021, her novel *Redemption* was almost complete, and she was in the process of tying up loose ends. Unfortunately, she ran out of time.

Leah Naess and Don Metzler, members of Karen's writing critique group, were familiar with the story that Karen was writing.

Together, Don and Leah put the finishing touches on *Redemption*, in exactly the way that they believe Karen would have done.

Karen's ashes reside in Rocky Mountain National Park and her voice and spirit live on in this novel.

To learn more about Karen, please visit her website at www.KarenStarkins.com.

Made in the USA
Las Vegas, NV
06 May 2024